KIDNAPPED

BOOK THREE:
THE RESCUE

GORDON KORMAN
TAKES YOU TO THE EDGE OF ADVENTURE

WWW.SCHOLASTIC.COM
WWW.GORDONKORMAN.COM

GORDON KORMAN

KIDNAPPED

BOOK THREE

THE RESCUE

AN
APPLE
PAPERBACK

SCHOLASTIC INC.

New York   Toronto   London   Auckland   Sydney
Mexico City   New Delhi   Hong Kong   Buenos Aires

For Leo

ISBN 0-439-84779-6

12 11 10 9 8 7 6 5 4   7 8 9 10 11/0

Printed in the U.S.A.   40

First printing, September 2006

PROLOGUE

NATIONAL WEATHER SERVICE: WASHINGTON, D.C.
10:53 P.M. E.D.T.
BLIZZARD WARNING

A MAJOR WINTER STORM SYSTEM WILL MOVE
THROUGH THE APPALACHIAN AND BLUE RIDGE
MOUNTAINS OF WESTERN VIRGINIA TONIGHT
THROUGH MIDDAY TUESDAY . . . LIGHT SNOW WILL
BECOME HEAVY . . . ACCOMPANIED BY POWER-
FUL WIND GUSTS OF 40–50 MILES PER HOUR TO
CREATE BLIZZARD CONDITIONS . . . 18–24 INCHES
EXPECTED AT ELEVATIONS ABOVE 2,000 FEET . . .
ALONG WITH WHITEOUT AND NEAR-ZERO VISIBIL-
ITY. . . .

A BLIZZARD WARNING MEANS SEVERE WINTER
WEATHER CONDITIONS ARE EXPECTED OR OCCUR-
RING . . . ONLY TRAVEL IN AN EMERGENCY . . . WITH
AN EXTRA FLASHLIGHT . . . FOOD . . . AND WATER
IN YOUR VEHICLE . . . UNDER NO CIRCUMSTANCES
VENTURE OUTDOORS ON FOOT. . . .

1

Snow.

It was the last thing Meg Falconer wanted to see.

She was lost in the woods. In the mountains. In the dark. Every limping step brought a fresh detonation of pain from her sprained ankle. Her one possession besides the clothes on her back was the pocket nail file she had used to saw through the ropes that had bound her to a chair.

Her thoughts turned to her three kidnappers. They were probably searching for her — two of them, anyway. So she was lost *and* hunted.

It was pitch-dark — was there such a thing as pitch-white? All she could see was the snow, blowing and swirling around her.

She had tried to bed down for the night in a hollow under a fallen tree. But a toxic mixture of pain, cold, and fear had made sleep impossible. The snow had been the last straw. She had to put as much distance as possible between herself and her captors before the white coating on the forest floor created tracks for them to follow.

She looked down. Her sneaker prints were unmistakable in the inch of powder that already covered the ground. If the kidnappers picked up her trail, she was doomed. With her twisted ankle, she couldn't stay ahead of them for long.

She plodded through the trees, the furious racing of her mind every bit as turbulent as the roiling snow.

Come on, one foot in front of the other . . .

She'd been hooded when her captors had carried her to the cabin hideout. But the direction had definitely been *up*. Down, then, was the way to go. It wasn't exactly a map, or even a compass, but it was the only point of reference she had.

When is this lousy snow going to stop?

Suddenly — without warning — the forest was *gone*!

She couldn't see it; she *felt* it. The stronger wind, unblocked by trees; the absence of branches scratching at her skin.

I'm in the open!

Had she made it out of the woods and back to civilization? No — in civilization there would be lights. It was just as black as before. Only the dim disk of the moon glowed through the snowy overcast above.

She closed her eyes in a concerted effort to boost her night vision. It was only ten seconds, but it felt like forever — lids squeezed shut, counting patiently. When she opened them at last, she could *see* again. It was still dead dark, but she could distinguish the different textures of black on black.

She had not left the forest; it was still all around her. This was some kind of clearing — a stripe about thirty feet wide, cut straight through the woods.

A firebreak?

Maybe, but weren't fires more of a problem out west, where it was drier? Her gaze fixed on a tall, vertical shadow in the center of the opening. She frowned. Why would they take the trouble to clear-cut a stripe through dense forest and then leave one tree standing right in the middle?

She squinted at the ramrod-straight trunk. It did not bend or taper and had no branches.

That's not a tree; it's a telephone pole!

That was the purpose of this clearing — to run power and phone lines through to the other side of the mountains.

When the plan came to her, it was already fully formed. It wasn't actually her idea; its source was a book by her father.

In addition to his career as a criminologist, Dr. John Falconer was the author of a series of detective novels. In *Murder in the Mojave*, the hero, Mac Mulvey, has been stranded in the desert and left to die. Lost, snakebit, and parched beyond endurance, Mulvey stumbles across a line of electrical wires. With the nearest human being dozens of miles away, the intrepid detective finds a way to send out a distress call.

As Meg began to climb the pole, she couldn't help reflecting that Mulvey didn't have to do this in the dark. He had no trouble telling the harmless telephone cables from the deadly high-voltage lines that would electrocute her on contact.

The wood was wet from snow. She pressed the rubber soles of her sneakers against the pole to keep from sliding. The wind nipped harder—she was making progress, even though she couldn't see the ground below.

That's a good thing, she reminded herself. Meg didn't like heights. She was grateful that the darkness made it impossible to look down.

All at once, a barrage of ice-cold needles assailed her face, as a monster gust threatened to tear her loose and fling her into the night. She pressed her body against the wood and hung on.

Just keep climbing . . .

When the cold cable touched her face, she cried out in shock and nearly jumped off the pole.

Calm down, she scolded herself. *If it was live, you'd be dead already!*

Struggling to control her gasping breath and the

runaway pounding of her heart, Meg rallied her night vision once again. She could see the power lines, still a few feet above her. This was the telephone wire. Perfect.

In *Murder in the Mojave*, Mac Mulvey cuts the cable with a Swiss Army knife. But all Meg had was the nail file. Tightening her legs' grip on the pole, she held on with her left arm and began sawing at the wire with her right.

As the file cut into the plastic insulation, she wondered if the stress of the kidnapping had caused her to lose her mind. Why was she wasting precious time on a stunt from Dad's cheesy novel? Mac Mulvey was a made-up detective, and this moment was very, very real.

Yet—crazy but true—Mac Mulvey's tactics some-times worked. His wild antics had saved her on more occasions than she cared to remember—especially back when she and her brother, Aiden, had been fugitives.

The file was already through the coating. She could feel it biting into the wire.

Her left leg was falling asleep. She shifted her position but didn't dare risk losing her purchase on the pole. She blinked the ice crystals out of her eyes. Was it snowing harder?

Concentrate! she ordered herself.

The wire was tough, but she could feel the metallic

filaments separating under the sawing action. At last, the cable broke in two.

She fought off the urge to cheer. This wasn't over yet. In *Murder in the Mojave*, Mulvey didn't just cut the telephone line; he used the severed ends to transmit a distress call in Morse code.

With the file, she carved away a few inches of insulation from each of the broken pieces, exposing the shiny wire inside. Then she began to tap the tips together, spelling out the code for SOS.

Dot-dot-dot . . . dash-dash-dash . . . dot-dot-dot . . .

She breathed a silent apology to anybody who might be trying to dial 911 along the line.

Like anybody else's emergency is bigger than mine right now!

A thought nagged at her. Dad himself had admitted that the adventures of his detective hero had never been tested. She ought to feel like an idiot thirty feet up a pole in the middle of the night in a snowstorm.

Dot-dot-dot . . . dash-dash-dash . . . dot-dot-dot . . .

She prayed that Mac Mulvey had one more miracle left for her.

Aiden Falconer stared at the large order of chili nachos on the table in front of him. He had not eaten in forty hours of intense pressure and heart-stopping effort. Most draining of all was the minute-to-minute gut-twisting dread that had been his constant companion since Meg had been kidnapped a week before.

FBI agent Emmanuel Harris peered at him over a hot cup of coffee big enough to float a battleship inside. "The best thing about nachos—even a truck stop can't ruin them."

Aiden pushed the plate away. "I told you—I'm not hungry."

But he was. Ravenous, in fact. Did that make him a horrible person, to be so keen on eating at a time like this? Was it disloyal to Meg to think nothing had ever smelled as delicious as these nachos?

"Doesn't help your sister if you starve," Harris said reasonably. He selected a jalapeño-laden chip and washed it down with a swig of coffee.

Aiden checked the clock over the counter: 11:35. They had been driving for at least a couple of hours. Three more would probably get them home.

Home. The thought should have cheered him. The embrace of his parents; a real night's sleep in his own bed. But Aiden believed he was his sister's only chance.

When I walk in the house, I'm giving up on her.

"It doesn't make sense," he mused aloud. "The kidnappers sent a message upping the ransom to three million. Why hasn't anybody heard from them since then?"

The agent shrugged. "Could be lots of reasons."

Aiden shook his head. "If this was really about ransom, they'd want to get their money and get lost. Something's wrong. We shouldn't be going back. We should be searching for Meg right now."

Harris sighed. "We've been through this already. The trail is stone-cold."

"You don't even care," Aiden said bitterly. "This isn't your case anymore."

Aiden had no love for Harris. But Harris's replacement, Mike Sorenson, was a do-nothing agent who wouldn't blow his nose without consulting the FBI manual first. Did a guy like that have a prayer of finding Meg?

Not unless her captors drop her on the doorstep and ring the bell. . . .

Harris chugged the rest of his huge coffee in three titanic gulps. "Look—that wasn't my decision. But if I were in Mike Sorenson's chair right now, we'd still be going home. It's best for you and it's best for your sister. The last thing this investigation needs is *two* Falconers to rescue. Now, are you going to eat or what?"

Reluctantly, Aiden took a few bites. It couldn't hurt to maintain his strength. The question loomed: Maintain his strength for what? More than once he'd considered ditching Harris and going after Meg on his own.

The last time I tried that, I almost got myself killed. . . .

Besides, the agent was watching him like a hawk.

When Aiden followed Harris back to the Trailblazer, he knew he'd never make a break for it. That was the truly awful part of this.

I'm bailing out on Meg.

At no time—not even the day his parents were wrongly convicted of treason—had Aiden Falconer felt so utterly, hopelessly miserable.

Flurries danced around the SUV as it pulled back onto the highway—light snow, nothing like the blizzard that had been predicted for the mountains. To make an unpleasant trip even more so, Harris monitored the local police radio as they drove. Not that Aiden was in the mood to count down the top forty with Casey Kasem. But reports of snowplows, road sanders, slippery conditions, and power and phone outages only seemed to make his melancholy worse.

The telephone problems were in Alberta County, where Aiden and Harris had just come from.

"Ice on the wires?" queried the dispatcher.

"Not likely," came the reply from the telephone lineman. "The connection kept cutting in and out over a period of ten minutes or so."

"Probably just the wind," the dispatcher suggested.

"Not any wind I ever heard of," the lineman told him. "It was fast and regular, like a person playing with the wires. Definitely not random."

The dispatcher sounded bewildered. "You think we've got a Good Samaritan—some clown trying to fix the wire?"

"No way," said the lineman. "We've pinpointed the break. It's in a mountain pass. There's nobody up there—not in this weather."

"Then what could it be?"

Aiden thought his heart might burst through his rib cage. "*SOS!*"

Startled, Harris struggled to keep his eyes on the road. "What are you talking about?"

"The phone interruption!" Aiden explained breathlessly. "SOS in Morse code! It's *Meg*!"

In a squeal of tires on wet pavement, the Trailblazer

pulled over and rolled to a stop on the soft shoulder. Harris wheeled around to his young passenger. "Convince me."

"It's from one of my father's books. Mac Mulvey cuts a telephone wire so he can tap out SOS in Morse code. We used stuff from the books a million times when we were fugitives. She's alive! She must have gotten away from her kidnappers and now she's calling for help!"

Harris looked him straight in the eye. "This is the truth, right? You're not jerking me around?"

"If she's free to send that SOS," Aiden said breathlessly, "that means she's lost in the mountains with a blizzard on the way!"

The Trailblazer screeched across four lanes of traffic in a highly illegal U-turn.

3

Meg ran through the worsening storm, following the clear-cut zone around the telephone wires. The decision to jog had nothing to do with speed. The only way to forget the pain in her ankle was to keep it hurting.

The effort also helped her stay warm. Warm*er*, anyway. Her sneakers were soaked. Her feet felt as if they'd been dipped in a liquid nitrogen bath. She was losing the battle of brushing snow off her clothes.

It had been at least a couple of hours since she'd sent out her Mac Mulvey distress call. She'd made it down one mountain and partway up the opposite slope. Icy buildup frosted her hair and accumulated on her eyebrows. Meltwater trickled down from her neckline, frigid against her bare skin.

She kept moving, as if trying to outrun the paralyzing cold. These power lines had to lead somewhere eventually — to a town, a city, even a transformer station with a night watchman. All she needed was a place to get warm and a telephone to call the police.

The wind was howling, bringing with it a solid wall of

snow. It was so loud that she didn't hear the sound of the engine until it was almost upon her. When the vehicle crested the rise, the headlight was like a supernova — so blindingly bright that it nearly knocked her over. Even more intense was the realization that came with it.

The phone company! They got my SOS!

She scrambled toward the beam, slipping and sliding, waving her arms to attract the driver's attention.

"Over here!"

She could see the ATV now — some sort of three-wheeler, like a tricked-out tricycle. Its huge tires kicked up snow and mud as it roared down on her.

"Thank you!" Meg shouted, rushing to meet it. There was an unreality to the notion that her ordeal was so suddenly *over*. The kidnapping, the nightmare —

The ATV jounced to the left, momentarily freeing Meg's eyes from the headlight's brilliance. For a split second, she got a good look at the vehicle's riders. In that electric instant, two things became devastatingly clear to her:

1. This was not the telephone company responding to her SOS, and

2. Her captors had found her once again.

The kidnapper she called Spidey was at the handlebars. Tiger's arms were wrapped around his midsection. Tiger was calling to her. What was the woman saying?

"Come with us if you want to live . . ."

Meg didn't stick around for the rest. She was already sprinting for the cover of the trees, the storm forgotten. In a spray of dirty slush, the big tires spun, and the ATV lurched after her.

She hit the forest running, threading her way through the trunks, hurdling roots. Her speed impressed her — until she realized why she was having so much success navigating the treacherous terrain —

I can see where I'm going!

And that meant . . .

She risked a backward glance. The ATV was plowing through the woods, its compact three-wheel design allowing it to slip between trees, crunching underbrush and bouncing over rocks. The headlight illuminated the silvery scene, glittering with snowflakes. Spidey and Tiger crouched in the saddle, bent low to avoid the clawing of branches. They couldn't drive very fast in such awkward quarters. But it wouldn't take much to outrun Meg — frozen, exhausted, and favoring a sprained ankle.

If I can get away from the light, they won't be able to see me!

Planting her good leg, she turned sharply, hustling out of the headlight's spill. The plan succeeded too well. She got only three strides in the blackness before a tree limb struck her forehead and down she went. Dazed, she scrambled up just as the beam fixed on her again.

"Margaret!" came Tiger's shout. "You'll never make it alone!"

Meg staggered away, head and ankle throbbing. *Maybe not*, she thought grimly. *But anything's better than going back with you.*

She picked her way through the trees, squeezing through gaps too narrow for the ATV. Somehow, Spidey managed to detour around the obstacles and stay on her tail.

There must be some way to lose them!

With the engine's clamor drowning out all other sound, Meg had no advance warning of the stream until she'd almost tumbled down the rocky embankment. She put on the brakes, sizing up the rushing water ten feet below. It seemed to be about waist-deep — not exactly a raging river. But in these conditions, it might as well have been. A full-body soaking in icy water would mean guaranteed hypothermia!

The three-wheeler swerved around a stump, and the bouncing headlight beam showed her the solution. A hundred yards away, a tree had toppled across the stream, forming a bridge to the other side. No ATV could ever follow her across that.

The thought of escape gave her feet wings, and she

raced to the fallen log. Her first thought was to tightrope-walk across. But one step on the soft, rotting wood made her ease herself down to a careful crawl. The trunk was eight inches in diameter, knobby and uneven, bobbing with her movements. Gritting her teeth, she shuffled forward, inch by inch. The opposite bank, thirty feet away, might as well have been another continent.

Keep moving!

Suddenly, her knees slipped on the snow-slick bark, and she was falling. Desperately, she clamped onto the trunk with her arms and ankles. She was halfway across, suspended over the cascading stream. She could hear the babble of the water—

Wait—why can I hear it?

And the terrifying answer: *The motor's off! They've stopped!*

The kidnappers jumped from the ATV and ran to the toppled tree. "Hold on, Margaret," Tiger shouted. "We're coming for you."

It was the kind of talk Meg had learned to expect from Tiger—helpful and encouraging on the surface, concealing a sinister core.

"Leave the light on!" instructed Spidey. The tree lurched as he crawled out onto the span. In a few more seconds, he would be upon her.

The thought channeled hidden stores of strength to

Meg's arms. She heaved herself back on top of the log and scrambled for freedom. The kidnapper clambered after her, barely a body-length behind.

What am I going to do when I get to the other side? I'll never outrun him. . . .

Her eyes fell on the stub of what had once been a tree branch. It was at the end of the span, pressed against the rocky ledge, holding the fallen trunk in place. She flung herself onto the opposite bank and began kicking at the truncated limb with her heel.

Spidey stared at her in outrage. "Don't even think about —"

With a snap, the piece broke off. Without the stub acting as a brake, the log rolled over on its side. With a howl of anger, Spidey was pitched free, plunging with a tremendous splash in the stream.

Meg couldn't resist wasting precious seconds, savoring the sight of this horrible criminal cursing and thrashing around in the glacial water. The kidnappers could not follow her now. They had to get Spidey warm and dry before they could resume the chase.

"Give it up, Margaret." Tiger's gaze was even colder than what her partner was enduring. "You know you'll never survive out here."

There was one thing worse than recapture: The notion that Tiger, terrible as she was, might be telling the truth.

4

Welcome to the Blog Hog
News, Opinions, and Whatnot
www.bloghog.usa

ATTENTION BLOGOSPHERE—HELP SAVE MEG
FALCONER!
URGENT CALL FOR DONATIONS

The FBI is playing games with Meg Falconer's life. Does
anybody honestly believe a 7th-grade girl would be a target for kidnapping if her parents hadn't been branded
as traitors? Never mind that the Falconers were innocent—the feds themselves admitted that after the parents had spent more than a year in prison.

Now the Bureau refuses to come up with 1 cent of the
$3-million ransom, despite the fact that the kidnappers
have threatened to kill their young hostage if the money
is not paid.

This is your chance to show the FBI that we're sick of the pain and misery caused by their bumbling. If we can raise $3 million, we can bring Meg Falconer home. Give what you can to save that little girl. Do it for a shattered family that has already suffered enough. Do it to show the government the true meaning of justice. Do it for an innocent child who just spent her 12th birthday in captivity, so she'll have more birthdays to celebrate in the future.

Agent Mike Sorenson swiveled his laptop around so the Falconers could see the web page. "What do you have to say about this?"

Dr. John Falconer cleared his throat carefully. "Well, you know that Rufus Sehorn has taken a special interest in Meg's kidnapping on his site—"

"He's supposed to be talking about the *reward*," Sorenson interrupted. "I don't see a word about it."

"A ten-thousand-dollar reward is a drop in the bucket," John argued. "The only way to get serious about bringing Meg home is to raise that ransom. We're very grateful to Rufus for using *bloghog.usa* to do it."

"The FBI doesn't sanction this," the agent said primly. "It's the policy of the U.S. government never to pay off or negotiate with kidnappers."

Louise Falconer spoke up, her voice firm. "You don't have any children, Agent Sorenson. If you did, you'd understand that we have to try absolutely everything to help our daughter, and that means *everything*. We didn't ask Rufus to do this for us—he came up with the idea on his own. As far as I'm concerned, that man has been sent straight from heaven. He's working night and day for us, while our own government has basically thrown in the towel."

It was a no-win situation. Sorenson would never convince the Falconers that he was doing everything he could. In a week-old abduction with no other leads, FBI procedure was to play a waiting game. Shouldn't two criminology professors understand that?

Besides, no one could say he wasn't going the extra mile for this case. It was two-thirty in the morning, and here he was, waiting up with the parents for Emmanuel Harris to bring their son home.

He shrugged into his overcoat and stepped outside, directing a slight nod to the undercover agent in the sedan parked at the curb. Where was Harris? There were reports of snow in the mountains, but Sorenson wasn't sure where or how much.

The thought had barely entered his mind when his cell phone rang. Harris's number appeared on the caller ID.

"Harris—where are you?"

The response was the last thing Agent Mike Sorenson had expected to hear:

"I'm looking for a place to rent a snowmobile."

Agent Harris had suspected his plan might not be a hit with Sorenson.

"What are you talking about?" Sorenson's voice demanded over the handset. "Where's Aiden Falconer?"

"Relax," said Harris. "He's right next to me in the car. He's okay."

Agent and runaway were in the Trailblazer, four-wheeling through heavy snow on a winding road in the Appalachian Mountains. They had just come from an isolated power company substation. Both had watched as a satellite photograph crept out of the printer—the exact spot of the interruption in the telephone lines.

Aiden had been strangely disappointed by the picture. What had he expected to see—Meg standing under the pole, waving and smiling? Actually, he couldn't see anything through the blur of cloud cover and snow. It had taken the station tech to point out the dangling wires, faint white threads on the infrared image.

Still, those threads were all he had of his sister. He clutched the slick paper and would not let go. Not until the real Meg was home, safe and sound.

"We've got a fresh lead," Harris went on. He told Sorenson about the odd interruptions detected by the phone company.

"It's a broken cable!" Sorenson interrupted angrily. "High winds, falling branches, ice buildup—there are a hundred possible explanations!"

"Not according to the field people at the substation. Definitely man-made, they say. And get this—one of the father's novels features a hero who taps out a message in Morse code using broken telephone wires."

"Novels?" repeated Sorenson.

"The father is an author, and the kids sometimes put his stories into action when the chips are down." The Trailblazer skidded on the icy pavement as Harris steered into the circular drive of a ski lodge. "It's worth looking into."

"This is *my* case!" Sorenson asserted. "*I* decide what's worth looking into!"

"I'll let you know if we come up with anything."

"No! I'm telling you to turn around and come home!"

"Maybe I should take some vacation time," Harris mused. "Do some snowmobiling in the mountains—"

"You're disobeying a direct order and putting a fifteen-year-old boy in danger!" Sorenson accused.

"It's not danger when you follow the buddy system. He's my buddy."

The SUV skidded to a halt at the main entrance, and Harris shut the flip phone. He skewered Aiden with a razor-sharp glare. "You'd better be right about this."

For the very first time, Aiden looked at the man who'd imprisoned his parents and did not see an enemy. "Thank you for believing me," he said.

Harris unfolded his six-foot-seven-inch frame out the driver-side door. "Let's go do this before Sorenson tells the Bureau to cancel my credit card."

The peace and quiet of the ski lodge was shattered when Harris threw open the front door and bounded in with Aiden in tow. "We'll need a snowmobile and two ski suits, along with goggles, boots, gloves—the works!"

"Sorry, mister," the desk clerk told him. "Our day-rental counter doesn't open until seven."

The agent took out an ID wallet and flashed a badge. The initials were unmistakable—FBI.

"Wake up the manager."

5

One foot in front of the other . . .

It was all the plan Meg had left. She limped through the snow, shivering from cold and the leftover shock from her near miss. She remained under cover of the woods. Dumping Spidey in the drink had bought her time, nothing more. The kidnappers would come after her again, once he'd changed into dry clothes.

I could put them both in prison for a long time.

Her thoughts turned to Mickey, the third captor. True, he was a criminal, but Meg had never really considered the twenty-year-old a bad person. Mickey had only signed on to the kidnapping plot because he was desperate for money to help a younger brother who was in trouble with the law.

Most important, Mickey had made it possible for Meg to escape from the mountain cabin where she'd been held. Who knew what kind of shape she'd be in if he hadn't acted?

Warmer, drier, and a lot less tired and hungry!

But not free — and that made all the difference. No

matter how exhausted and miserable she might have been, if she walked far enough—staying parallel to the power lines—sooner or later she would reach help.

Suddenly, an overpowering rush of wind knocked her off her feet and tossed her into the snow.

She was more surprised than hurt. *Where did that come from?*

She picked herself up into a world she barely recognized. Millions of wind-driven snowflakes blurred into a curtain of chaotic white. It was a white that she *felt* rather than saw. In fact, she couldn't see anything, not even trees that were only a few feet away.

Another gust sent her stumbling backward into a trunk. She clamped her arms around it to stabilize herself. Terror gripped her. Which direction had she been going? She was surrounded on all sides by whiteout conditions. Everything depended on following the path of the power lines—

And I don't have the faintest idea which way that is.

Never before had she felt so completely disoriented. It was as if she'd been suddenly transported to the emptiness of intergalactic space—with no sense of left or right, here or there.

She spun helplessly. All directions looked equally possible—and equally wrong. Closing her eyes, she tried to call up some kind of internal compass. She took three steps and bounced off another tree, all but invisible in the boiling white.

The wind tore through the woods, piercing her body with cold. It propelled the snow into her with such force that every flake stung her face like a tiny ice needle. Doggedly, she leaned into the storm. It felt as if the tempest could blow her over at any moment.

Each step was an effort now, a struggle against the gale. Or was the snow the problem — blowing, drifting, deeper around her legs every minute? Worst of all was the thought that she didn't know if she was going the right way — or *any* way for that matter. She could very well be walking in circles.

Even more hobbling than the storm was the reality that pressed down on her: In this weather, there was no telling how long it would take her to make it to civilization. There was no telling if she would make it to civilization at all.

There was no telling whether Meg Falconer was going to live or die.

6

Aiden and Harris were on the snowmobile, heading up the side of a mountain, when the blizzard hit.

The first onslaught nearly flung Aiden clear off the machine. The barrage reminded him of the time he'd been hit by a huge wave while bodysurfing — a manhandling force of nature. He tightened his grip on Harris's ski suit and ducked low, using the driver as a windbreak. It was like being in a tunnel, dense snow blasting past on all sides. The brilliant halogen headlight that had illuminated the line of telephone poles now showed nothing but a wall of moving white.

Harris slowed but did not stop. "You okay back there?" he bellowed over his shoulder. The words were barely audible over the Ski-Doo's engine.

Aiden's own well-being was the last thing on his mind. "If it's this bad for us —"

A sharp gust took his breath away, but the train of thought wasn't hard to follow. They were protected by down-filled ski suits, goggles, and Gore-Tex boots and gloves. Meg had none of these things.

The agent read his concern. "We can't be sure of anything yet!"

Aiden pressed into Harris's back and tried to convince himself that his sister had taken cover somewhere, away from the wrath of this brutal blizzard. He even toyed with the awful wish that he'd been wrong about the Mac Mulvey distress call. That would put Meg still in the hands of her kidnappers, but at least she'd be safe from the storm.

This is the kind of weather people die in. . . .

Harris hunched over the console, staring into the headlight beam in a dogged attempt to see through the airborne porridge.

When the tree trunk came into view, it seemed to explode out of the snow, hurtling toward them from point-blank range. Frantically, Harris yanked on the handlebars with all the strength in his six-foot-seven frame. For a split second, Aiden was positive the Ski-Doo would flip over. At the last second, the treads bit into the snow, and the machine righted itself, veering away from the woods, collision, and disaster.

Aiden tried to calm the drum-solo beating of his heart into a stable rhythm. Navigation should have been simple — follow the clear-cut until the agent's handheld GPS system told them they had reached the coordinates of the broken cable. But in zero visibility, simply maintaining a straight line was next to impossible. Harris's grip on the controls was so tight that his body felt carved from granite.

Suddenly, the engine of the Ski-Doo went silent.

"What happened?" Aiden demanded as they glided, losing speed. "Why are we stopping?"

"We're here," Harris announced over his shoulder.

"No we're not! We're nowhere!"

With a *whump*, the Ski-Doo coasted into the base of a telephone pole that appeared out of nowhere.

When Aiden got up, the wind very nearly knocked him off his feet. Never in his fifteen years had he experienced this kind of blizzard. The air was solid snow. Every breath left him choking on a mouthful of slush.

"What now?" he managed.

Harris tossed a flashlight to Aiden and switched on his own. With a groan, the agent began to shinny up the wet pole, the nylon fabric of his ski suit slipping and sliding.

"Wait—she can't still be up there, can she?" Aiden stepped back for a better look and something touched his face.

He reached out and grabbed it—the severed end of a phone cable, hanging down from the line above.

"I've got it!" he shouted. "Agent Harris—I found the wire!"

He held it to his chest. *Meg cut this.* The idea of touching something his sister had touched was practically magic.

Harris jumped down and examined the cable. "Bingo."

"But the SOS was hours ago," Aiden said dejectedly. "She could be miles away."

Harris played his flashlight across the white on white. "No tracks," he commented. "Everything would be long buried by now."

And then the beam fell on an area of shallower snow at the edge of the trees on the lee side of the storm. The wind had blown much of the powder into the clearing, so the cover was only a few inches here.

You couldn't call them footprints — not anymore. But there was no question that they once had been. Ever-so-slight oval depressions at regular intervals. Left, right, left, right.

"I'd say that's just about the shoe size of a twelve-year-old girl," Harris said.

"Yeah, but which way was she heading?" asked Aiden. "Are the tracks coming or going?"

"Impossible to tell," the agent decided. "We can only follow them into the woods. They disappear in the deeper snow."

"But what if that's the wrong direction?"

Harris was already striding back to the Ski-Doo. "If

we don't find her, maybe we'll find what she's running from. Either way, we'll know more than we do now."

The tall man crammed his long legs into the machine, and Aiden took his place at the rear. The engine roared to life in a cloud of ice crystals.

They entered the forest, driving much more slowly. The faint tracks threaded a slalom course through the trees.

Aiden held on to Harris and to this hope: If they could pinpoint a broken wire in a far-flung wilderness in the middle of a blizzard, surely they still had a chance of locating his sister.

He could only pray she was alive when they finally found her.

7

Meg's left leg went suddenly numb and buckled, throwing her full-length into the snow. The fall wasn't bad — at this point, the forest floor was covered with an eighteen-inch cushion of powder. But the true meaning of what was happening to her could not be denied.

My body is shutting down, she thought clinically, as if she were talking about a patient in the hospital. It was happening part by part, system by system, as cold and fatigue whittled away at her. Her fingers were like icicles. Her ears hurt. Even the shivering itself was exhausting. It made her breathing shallow and irregular. Most alarming of all, there were times where it felt like she was asleep on her feet.

Tiger was right, she reflected grudgingly. *I'll never survive out here on my own.*

She could picture it: A spill just like this one, and she might be too bone-weary to get up. In these conditions, nothing could be more lethal than relaxing. Movement was the only thing providing what little warmth she had.

She scrambled upright and stood for a moment, trying to massage some life into her left leg. Scariest of all was how easy it would have been to fall asleep down there. At the rate it was snowing, she would have been buried in an hour.

She limped along, held together by sheer stubbornness. She was moving, but toward what? She had long since given up on the idea of getting anywhere in this weather.

She shook herself like a wet dog in an attempt to clear her foggy thoughts. She was walking to stay alive, and staying alive to keep walking. That didn't make sense, did it?

Confusion — she had read somewhere that it was one of the signs of hypothermia. She was in real trouble here. Stopping was not an option. But in a corner of her mind, she understood that she couldn't keep going forever.

It might have been the zero visibility, or maybe the fact that her eyes were partly shut. Whatever the reason, she never saw the low rock ledge until her jaw banged into it. She wasn't going very fast, but in her depleted state, the blow was like being hit in the face with a cannonball. She dropped where she stood and lay there in a heap, knowing that something major had changed.

I can't get up!

She could not seem to pull herself to one knee. Her

mind was issuing the right commands, but her body wasn't responding.

Her first instinct was anger. This was a faulty equipment problem.

Give it a minute. Shut down. Reboot . . .

She waited, counting off thirty seconds. Any longer than that would have put her life in danger. Then she managed to get to all fours but could not progress further.

Unbelievable! She had survived a kidnapping—*only to freeze to death on the side of a mountain!*

Somehow, admitting this to herself—that this was very likely the end—brought out the iron will that was at the core of her character. She began to crawl, her knees plowing through deep snow, moving by inches, but moving. It was the ultimate meaningless gesture—a snail trying to cross a vast continent. There was no hope left, only effort. She struggled purely out of a mule-headed refusal to give up, even though the final result was no longer in doubt.

Her feelings were jumbled but centered on a single theme: She would never see her family again. Mom and Dad suffering in prison had turned out to be merely a warm-up for greater sorrows to come. The Falconers had fought hard to be together, but no amount of fighting could overcome death.

Suddenly, she stopped crawling, vaguely aware that something was different. Wrong.

It's not snowing anymore!

Had the storm ended? In the utter blackness, she probed around with her hands. The amazing thing was not what she found, but what she didn't.

Where's the snow? A blizzard can stop, but a foot and a half of powder doesn't disappear in the blink of an eye.

She reached up to feel for falling snow and hit solid rock. The ledge! The one she'd stumbled into and knocked herself silly. Somehow, she must have clambered *under* it! The storm was still howling, but she was sheltered.

She crept forward, exploring with her fingers. Dead leaves crackled.

They're dry! Cold but dry!

Had she blundered into a cave? She bumped up against a barrier. No, it seemed to be a natural stone alcove, protected by an overhanging roof. And because of the direction of the wind, the storm wasn't blowing in.

She slithered to the deepest corner of the niche and backed herself against the frigid rock. She began to gather armloads of the dry leaves, hoping to cover herself for warmth. The leaves and twigs were so frigid that they merely added to her miseries. Still, her spot was a whole lot more comfortable than battling the weather in the open.

She came to a decision. She would wait out the blizzard in here, massaging herself to keep warm. If she could stay awake, stay active, she had a chance.

Her jeans were frozen solid. With her fingernails, she tried to break off some of the ice to soften the fabric. That was when she found the nail file in her pocket, which aided in her self-defrosting.

The idea came from there. She could use the file to write with, to scratch a few words into the stone. If she didn't make it, at least Mom and Dad and Aiden would know she'd been thinking about them.

The message would have to be short. She wasn't going to compose *The Lord of the Rings* with a nail file on a rock in the dark. She finally decided on: MOM, DAD, AIDEN—LOVE YOU ALWAYS, MEG.

She reached up to scrape the first letter into the alcove — M for MOM. The stroke almost paralyzed her with shock.

The friction of file against stone produced a shower of sparks.

It had been so many hours since she'd been exposed to light that the orange glow from the sparks was almost blinding.

She tried again, rubbing the flat of the file against the wall. More sparks, brighter this time.

Her mind made the leap. Sparks meant fire; fire meant heat; heat meant survival.

But what can I use for fuel? There's no dry wood around here!

She shifted, and her knee crunched in the bed of leaves. Of course! The leaves! They wouldn't burn for long, but they'd definitely burn. Any fire was better than no fire at all.

Operating by touch alone, she gathered together a pile of leaves at the base of the wall. Then she went to work with the file, raining down a cascade of sparks. All seemed to wink out before they found the kindling.

With a frown of exasperation, she began to scrape at a lower spot, closer to the pile. This area, however, must have been a different kind of rock. It produced only faint sparks, which did not catch.

At last, she returned to the original place on the wall. This time, though, she took a handful of the leaves and held them directly under the falling sparks. The glowing orange points landed delicately.

She wasn't sure if it came from instinct or Mac Mulvey—she began to blow on the smoldering leaves, not from above, but from below, creating a draft. The points glowed brighter and turned into tiny flames, dancing in her palm and growing. When she dropped the burning kindling into the larger pile, it was a fire—a real one, sizzling a little in the cold and beginning to crackle.

The warmth of it on her hands, her entire body, created a woozy joy that was nothing short of heaven.

With the heat came light, and a real view of her surroundings. She was tucked under a stone ledge about four feet off the ground. Through the opening, she could see the storm still raging outside. In alarm, she noted how quickly the leaves were turning to ash. In no time, the fire would be out. Frantically, she scoured her alcove, feeding every leaf and twig into the blaze. Still, she could tell she'd only bought herself a few minutes.

Now that she had heat, the notion of losing it was unthinkable. She even considered burning some of her clothes — anything to keep herself bathed in this beautiful warmth.

Don't be crazy! If you burn your clothes, you'll just freeze twice as fast when the fire's gone.

Her eyes scanned the pool of light outside her shelter. Wood! Lots of it. Dead branches protruded from the drifting snow. They were wet, but the flames would dry them. Then they would burn for a long time.

Still crawling, she ventured to the edge of her niche and began to gather in the plentiful fuel supply. The thickest branches were the best because the wetness of the snow could not have penetrated down to the core.

She selected two and placed them carefully on the blazing leaves. The hiss frightened her. Thick dense smoke filled the alcove and poured out into the night. The flames died down to almost nothing.

"Don't go out! Don't go out!" she begged aloud. Flat on her stomach, she blew gently, praying that she had not extinguished her own fire. Slowly, the hissing died away and the smoke eased. Fingers of flame began to lick around the logs, engulfing them.

"Yes!" It was like one of her father's fires those winter Sundays — a monumental hassle to build, yet a pleasure to enjoy.

Heat surrounded her, feeding strength into her weakened body. With the sense of well-being came an overpowering drowsiness. She tried to wrestle it away and went so far as to slap her own face. But even as she battled, she knew that nothing could have kept her awake at that moment.

. . . no sleep . . . too dangerous . . .

She could not complete the thought before slumber claimed her.

The faint tracks had long since disappeared, but Harris and Aiden forged on through the blizzard. They picked a squiggly course among the trees, following what they hoped was the line the footsteps had been taking. With a whiteout all around, their only navigation aid was the built-in compass on the snowmobile. That and their desire not to wrap their rented craft around an evergreen, or roll it down the mountain.

The cold was taking its toll on Aiden, but not half as much as the infernal vibration of the machine. There were people, he knew, who rode these things for fun. He couldn't imagine it. And being hemmed in on all sides by an impenetrable curtain of gale-driven snow didn't make the ride any more pleasant.

As bad as it was for Aiden, it had to be worse for Harris. He sat tall in the saddle, with the full force of the storm battering him head-on, frosting his goggles white. He was tough, this man from the FBI. Never once had he suggested that they turn back.

The thud jolted the Ski-Doo, tipping Aiden off into the snow. When he looked up, wood was flying in all directions, raining down on him. A piece struck his cheek, and he saw stars.

What happened? Did we hit a tree?

No. This was cut wood—firewood. He heard Harris curse, and then the motor went dead.

"Aiden, are you okay? Where are you?"

Aiden struggled to his feet. Although the agent was close by, the only thing visible was his bobbing flashlight beam.

"I think we hit a woodpile," Aiden explained.

"You don't chop wood without a fireplace to burn it in," Harris agreed. "There must be a house here somewhere."

A house! Did that mean Meg might be inside? Was the end of this nightmare just yards away?

They wandered for a few minutes before a dark A-frame structure loomed out of the white. A log cabin, banked in snow.

Harris pulled Aiden beside him and intoned, "You don't go in there until I call you, got that?"

Aiden nodded silently.

From a zippered pocket, Harris took a small snub-nosed pistol. Holding it close to his chest, he reached forward and tried the door. It was unlocked. Silently, he swung it wide and stepped inside, ducking his head under the low frame.

Disobeying orders, Aiden followed a few steps behind him. If there was a chance Meg was in this house, he didn't want to be one second late in setting her free.

The cabin was tiny, and cold enough that Aiden could see his breath. A single candle burned on a table by a sofa. Stretched out there, wrapped in many blankets, lay a young man, fast asleep.

Scowling at Aiden, Harris motioned for him to be silent and then did a quick check of the small kitchen and lone bedroom. Satisfied that the sleeper was the cabin's sole occupant, he returned to the couch and snatched off the blankets.

"Okay, pal, rise and shine."

The young man was groggy. "Did you find her?" he mumbled. "Is she all right?"

There could be no doubt who he was talking about.

Harris grabbed the man by his collar and slammed him against the wall

"Where's Meg Falconer?"

The kidnapper Meg called Mickey came to sudden and total awareness. One thing was obvious: The two ski-suited intruders were not his missing accomplices.

"Who are you?"

"FBI!" Harris barked, pressing him harder against the planks. "Now where's the girl?"

The cornered kidnapper did the last thing Aiden expected. He burst into tears. "I — I helped her escape! I didn't know there was going to be a storm!"

It confirmed Aiden's worst fears. "I knew it! She's out there! She's lost in the blizzard!"

But the investigator in Harris was working full-tilt. "What do you mean you helped her escape?" As he spoke, he did a one-handed pat-down of his prisoner, coming up with a battered wallet. "What's your part in this" — Reading from the driver's license — "Sean Michael Antonino?"

Mickey — Sean — looked miserable. "I did it! I mean, I was with them when they grabbed her. But they lied! They said they were doing it for the money and they'd never hurt her — "

Harris's grip tightened convulsively. *"What did they do to her?"*

"Nothing!" Mickey said quickly. "But they were going to. That's why I helped her get away." In the flickering light of the candle, he recognized Harris's teen companion. "You're her brother — I'm sorry, man! It wasn't supposed to turn out this way! I only wanted the money to get a lawyer for my kid brother."

Harris shoved Mickey roughly onto the sofa. "Now you're going to need *two* lawyers! You'd better tell me everything about this kidnapping and the people who are in it with you!"

Mickey shrugged unhappily. The truth was he knew next to nothing about Spidey and Tiger, his accomplices. "They call themselves Joe and Marcelle—I'm not sure if those are real names. That was the whole plan. Nobody has much information, so we can't give the others up when it's over."

"That's not good enough," Harris snarled. "I want every detail from the beginning! I've had a rough night. And now's your last chance to convince me that yours shouldn't get even rougher!" He leaned in menacingly.

Aiden spoke up. "Agent Harris, cut it out! Can't you see he's the one who helped her?"

Harris scowled. "She wouldn't have needed help if it wasn't for him."

"Yeah, *then*. But he's on our side now."

The agent was exasperated. "I'm so lucky to have you here to tell me how to do my job! Yeah, he's on our side. They always switch sides when they're getting arrested! Unless you can read his mind—"

Aiden was adamant. "What was the first thing he said when he was still half asleep? 'Is she all right?' He cares about Meg."

"Oh, that's good enough for me!" Harris exclaimed sarcastically. But he backed off and returned the pistol to his zipper pocket. "All right, Sean. You said you let Meg escape because the other two were going to hurt her. What made you think that?"

"I looked on Joe's laptop," Mickey tried to explain. "He visits all those websites run by people who hate the Falconers — who think they're guilty and should be executed. It's really nasty stuff."

Harris looked pained. "I've seen it." He was the agent who had made the case against Aiden and Meg's parents. The so-called Falconer-haters, who would not accept the couple's innocence, were his fault. It was something he could never take back, the greatest mistake of his career.

Mickey went on. "And I thought, what if he's planning to kill her in order to take revenge on her parents? I had to get her away from him." His face fell. "But then it started snowing." He seemed about to cry again.

"And the others," Harris prompted. "They're out looking for her?"

The twenty-year-old nodded. "But that was hours ago. Anything could have happened in a storm like this. They could be dead, too!" His horrified eyes flew to Aiden. "Not that she's dead — "

Aiden clenched his teeth and tried to look stoic. The

possibility of Meg dying of exposure had occurred to him long before the words had passed Mickey's lips.

"Show me the computer," ordered Harris.

"The *computer?*" Aiden echoed. "Meg's out there in the storm! You're not going to find her on MapQuest!"

"The ransom demands were sent to the Blog Hog website by e-mail," the agent reasoned. "If this is the computer they came from, we need to check it out."

"Marcelle knows a guy who's an Internet expert," Mickey supplied. "He can bounce a message all over the world, make it impossible to trace."

"You can worry about that *later*!" Aiden insisted frantically. "The computer can wait; Meg can't!"

"Listen to me," Harris said earnestly. "I'm going to call the Forest Service to blanket these mountains with searchers. But in this weather, they're not going to do anything until daylight."

"But that could be hours!" Aiden protested.

"Just two. Look, I'm not trying to scare you, but there's something we have to face up to. If your sister's still alive, it's because she found shelter out there. A couple of hours won't make any difference if she's out of the storm. If not—"

There was no need for him to complete the sentence.

Daylight.

The sight of it was such a shock to Meg that she tried to scramble to her feet, only to whack her head on the low rock ceiling of the alcove.

"Ow!"

Reeling, she barely noticed the pain as the results of her self-inventory raced to her brain.

I'm alive! The biggest surprise in waking up was that she had woken up at all. Better yet, her arms and legs seemed to be in perfect working order. Even her sprained ankle didn't hurt so much.

She checked her fire and noted a pile of ash with a few still smoldering embers. There was even a tiny area of warmth surrounding it. There was no doubt in her mind that it had saved her life.

She crawled forward for a look outside.

And froze.

The fur was dark brown, almost black. The tail was stubby.

A groundhog, right? Let it be a groundhog!

She took stock of the broad back and powerful neck and shoulders.

A bodybuilding groundhog.

The creature grunted, rolled over, and lifted its shaggy head. The profile was unmistakable.

A bear.

Terrified, Meg backed away. Wary eyes watched her. The animal got to all fours and shook itself. Meg's fears ebbed slightly. This was not a fully-grown bear. It was a cub, roughly the size of a large bale of hay.

Small comfort. It was still a wild animal, still dangerous. One playful swat could knock her unconscious or rip open her chest. Baby though it was, the cub probably outweighed her by a lot.

"What are you doing here, Junior?" she mumbled nervously. "Shouldn't you be hibernating or something?"

She struggled to remember her fifth-grade science unit on bears. Not all hibernated, and even the hibernators weren't in a deep sleep all winter.

Maybe Junior got up for a drink of water and got lost in the blizzard.

Meg's heart turned over. A child separated from its family. It rang a bell. This cub was a fellow traveler, practically a Falconer bear.

"Let's hope we both make it home, kid."

Slowly, she backed out of the alcove and stood in snow

that measured well above her knees. The storm was over now, and the weather was clear except for a few flurries. She had no idea where she was, or how far she'd come from the clear-cut lane where the power lines marched. She only knew she had to find it and get going. Now that the blizzard had passed, Spidey and Tiger would be out searching for her again. And in two feet of snow, she was going to be leaving a trail that a blind man could follow.

Still facing the shelter that had preserved her life — you didn't turn your back on a bear, even a cute one — she reversed a few steps farther into the woods. In a matter of seconds, her jeans were every bit as wet as they had been last night when she'd dragged herself out of the blizzard.

The bear cub appeared under the rock ledge, watching her. Then it plunged into the fresh powder and took off after her, flailing limbs propelling it at an alarming speed.

Meg knew panic in its purest form. There was no fear quite like the fear of something that could eat you.

Don't run! she ordered herself. That was another fifth-grade science lesson. Bears had a chase reflex. If you tried to flee, they would stop at nothing to catch you.

The cub scrambled toward her but came no closer than twenty feet. There it stayed, rolling and frolicking in the snowdrifts, kicking up a spray. Almost — playing?

Not just playing—showing off!

It proved two things: First, the cub wasn't planning to attack her. Second, it preferred to keep a safe distance. It was as scared of her as she was of it. Which still didn't make it harmless. Somewhere, this thing had a mother. And that recalled rule number one from the fifth-grade unit: Never hang around a bear cub, because, sooner or later, a mama bear might show up.

Defying her own advice, she turned away from the cub and began to plow through the snow. Every time she paused to look back, the creature was still there, twenty feet back, following her.

She clapped her hands sharply. "Shoo!"

Junior dropped back a few more feet but kept coming.

It took two hours of hard slogging before the cub either grew exhausted or lost interest. By the time it was completely out of sight, Meg had already begun to miss it.

11

The Ski-Doo raced along the unplowed mountain road, its motor groaning under the weight of three people riding a machine built for two. Mickey was sandwiched between Harris and Aiden.

It was a precarious, almost impossible arrangement. Every bump and curve threatened to hurl Aiden overboard into a four-foot drift. It would have been much more balanced with the smaller teenager in the middle. But Harris refused to allow the kidnapper to ride on the end and perhaps have a chance to escape.

"Where's he going to go?" Aiden had argued. "You can't run through all this snow."

"I'm not going to run," Mickey promised. "I want to help find Meg and make things right."

"You're in a lot of trouble, mister," Harris reminded him. "You get points for cooperating, but you're still a part of this. You'd better pray we find that girl in one piece."

Making the ride even more treacherous was the fact that Harris was driving with one hand. The other was on his cell phone, which was getting spotty reception because of the mountains.

"Can you hear me?" he bellowed for at least the fifteenth time. "My name is Emmanuel Harris—I'm with the FBI! There's a girl lost in the woods—answer me! Are you there? Her last known coordinates—"

From around a blind curve came a flashing blue light. Beneath it roared a huge plow, pushing a wall of white seven feet high.

Harris heaved on the handlebars, and the Ski-doo veered sideways, skirting the angled blade by inches. A second later, a tidal wave of snow rolled over them, burying machine and riders.

Suddenly, Aiden realized that he could neither move nor breathe. He tried a swimming motion, but that only seemed to dig him in deeper. Then a large hand grabbed him by the fabric of his ski suit and hauled mightily. His head broke the surface in time for him to see the plow disappearing down the road in a cloud of airborne powder.

His rescuer, Harris, shouted after it. "Thanks for stopping to make sure we're okay!"

"I don't think he even saw us," commented Mickey, teeth chattering.

All three were as white as ghosts, and Mickey did not have the protection of modern ski gear.

The incident had its funny side, but it was no laughing matter. Every minute lost was that much more delay before Harris could get the Forest Service out searching for Meg.

It seemed to take forever for the three of them to dig out the Ski-Doo and get it on the road and running again. Even more serious was the discovery that Harris's cell phone was lost somewhere in the vast pile. Wasting more time looking for it was not an option.

With the road plowed, they drove along the shoulder. Mickey directed Harris to the tiny ski town the kidnappers had used for supplies. The place looked different under two feet of snow, but Aiden recognized it instantly.

"We were *here*!" he exclaimed in agony to Harris. "We were so close to finding her!" If only they hadn't left; if they had looked a little closer, tried a little harder, his sister might not be lost in the mountains right now, struggling or maybe even dead.

They crossed Route 119 and followed a winding drive downhill to a rustic-looking ski lodge.

"This is where we went for Internet access," Mickey explained. "To send messages through the secure e-mailer."

"I know the place," Aiden managed. It seemed like forever, but it was really only a couple of days since he had rocketed down the main ski hill on a stolen ten-speed bike. For all he knew, Meg's kidnappers had been just inside the lodge while he did battle with the hotel's snowmaking machinery.

Harris emitted an exhausted sigh. "My luck — wrong hotel."

The resort where he and Aiden had rented the Ski-doo and equipment was probably dozens of miles away. That was where the Trailblazer was parked. At some point, Harris would have to find it again, either driving the snowmobile, or in a rented pickup with the Ski-Doo on the flatbed. The mere thought of it made him wearier. But first things first.

The machine roared up to the front entrance. Harris leaped off, grabbed Aiden and Mickey, and shoved them ahead of him into the lobby. Once inside, he made a bee-line for a bank of pay phones, keeping a close watch on his two captives, who were huddled together, dripping meltwater on the carpet.

Agent Mike Sorenson stood in his T-shirt and boxers, lathering his face for his morning shave when the call came in.

"Harris, where are you? Where's Aiden Falconer?"

"He's standing about twenty feet away from me — right next to one of the kidnappers."

"One of the kidnappers?" Sorenson repeated. "Back up! What's going on?"

Harris delivered a quick update on everything that had happened since he and Aiden had left the power company substation and gone to rent the snowmobile. "We found the cabin where she was being held, and I arrested the guy who helped her escape. He's cooperating so far."

"Where's the girl?" Sorenson probed.

"Out there somewhere," Harris supplied grimly. "I've got the Forest Service looking for her. My prisoner says his two accomplices have been out after her all night. She could be with them now. To tell you the truth, I'm almost hoping for it." His voice dropped in volume. "I've got a bad feeling about this, Sorenson. We had a once-in-a-generation storm last night. If she was out in that, I figure it's at least fifty-fifty she didn't make it."

"Aw, jeez!" Sorenson groaned. "Have you got anything on the other two kidnappers?"

"My guy doesn't know much. Descriptions. First names, maybe phony. But I think I have the laptop they used to send the ransom e-mails. I've got it hooked up to an Internet connection here, and our tech people are examining it online."

"Good idea," Sorenson acknowledged. He had little tolerance for the way Harris had defied orders and horned in on an investigation that was none of his business. But he had to admit that this was a major break in the case. "I appreciate what you've done. I'm not sure how long it's going to take me to get out there. How are the roads?"

"They're plowing them now," Harris replied. "Trust me on that one."

"I'm on my way," Sorenson promised. "And when I get there, you can enjoy that vacation you were talking about."

There was a long silence. When Harris spoke again, he was obviously choosing his words carefully. "You're the lead. I respect that. But I'm not leaving. The Falconers are on my conscience. I won't abandon them until this is over, one way or the other."

Sorenson bit his lip and refused to be drawn into an argument. As the lead agent, he had every right to order Harris to back off. But he understood the big man's feelings about the family. It was every agent's nightmare to make the kind of mistake Harris had made with the Falconers.

He reached out and wrote the name BLUE VALLEY SKI RESORT with his finger on the fogged bathroom mirror.

"Thanks, Harris. I'll see you soon." He drew a deep breath. "What am I going to tell the parents?"

"Tell them that their son is safe," Harris advised. "And their daughter — I wish I could say."

12

Tired. Cold. Hungry.

That refrain marked the rhythm of Meg's tortured footsteps as she plowed through knee-deep snow and thigh-high drifts.

In a way, Meg Falconer had ceased to exist except for those three words. Her personality, her spirit had been whittled away. All that was left was what tormented her: exhaustion, hypothermia, starvation.

Earlier, she had seen a few birds feasting on some wild berries. When the little creatures didn't drop dead of poisoning, she had eaten a fistful of the tiny frozen fruits. They had thawed in her mouth to release a taste so nasty and so sour that she could feel her face crumple. Yet she had not left a single one on the branch. The birds would have to look elsewhere. They, at least, could fly.

Or had she hallucinated the birds? It was more than possible that her eyes were deceiving her. Her ears definitely were. A dozen times in the last few hours, she had distinctly heard her kidnappers crashing through the underbrush, pursuing her.

Of course, those noises in the bush could have been branches breaking under the weight of the snow. Or small animals—even her bear cub—following at a distance. Or the fevered imagination of a mind that was ceasing to function.

I'm losing it. . . .

Meg was no quitter. When she and Aiden had been fugitives, chased not just by police, but also a trained killer, she had never given up. When she had been kidnapped, she had not lost hope. Yet now the enemy was no human being, but nature itself. Nature couldn't be fought. No matter how far she slogged through this, nature could always conjure up more snow, more trees, more miles.

She crested a rise and looked down into the valley below for the city/town/village she had been praying to see. Just more of the same—white barren wilderness.

Then she noticed the smoke.

She was so startled that she lost her footing, pitched forward, and began to roll. She reached out frantically for some way to put on the brakes. There was nothing but many inches of fresh snow, a powdery slide bearing her downward. Her searching hands found no rock, no shrub, nothing to stop her descent.

As she picked up speed, the powder inundated her,

finding its way up every sleeve, into every pocket, through every seam. It was in her ears, up her nose.

Still, even tumbling out of control, her mind stayed focused on the smoke. *Did I really see it?*

Smoke meant fire; fire meant people.

She opened her mouth to call for help and was instantly gagged by a throatful of snow that stung her teeth and choked her.

As the slope began to level out, she was able to dig her sneakers into the more solid snow beneath the powder to slow her fall. She was frosted from head to toe, spitting and coughing, but unhurt as she scrambled to her feet.

Her mind might have been hazy before, but it was super-sharp now, concentrated like a laser beam on a single thought: the smoke. Had it been real? Or just a cloud? Or wishful thinking?

But there it was, rising into the chill air. Even more astonishing, she could now see the source of the plume. A tiny cottage, covered with snow, looking like a small square igloo.

On closer examination, there were eight or ten of these structures arranged in a loose semicircle in a clearing. Only one had smoke coming from the chimney.

Cabins! And at least one of them was occupied!

Heart leaping, she tried to break into a run, but the heavy snow put her flat on her face. Undaunted, she got up again and began to march toward this place of safety. Shelter, dry clothes, hot food, a telephone, rescue — all within reach.

I did it! I walked out of the mountains!

It was not until now, with the ordeal almost over, that she realized what a long shot it had always been for her to get to this moment.

As she stumbled into the clearing, she rehearsed what she was going to say to these people: *My name is Margaret Falconer, and I'm a kidnap victim. Call the police. . . .*

An ice-crusted sign read:

CABINS — WEEKLY — MONTHLY — SEASON

FIREPLACES — FREE CABLE TV

A boxy mound in front of the occupied cabin turned out to be a snow-buried car. There were no tracks in the powder. That meant the occupants were in!

As she moved to the door, she passed the single window in front of the cottage. The scene inside was a cozy domestic one. A woman sat in an easy chair, warming her feet by a roaring fire. A man leaned against the mantle. The couple was deep in conversation.

It was all very comfortable, except for one appalling detail—the two people were Spidey and Tiger.

Crushing disappointment mingled with instant terror. Meg jumped back from the window as if she'd been burned. Of all the cabins in all the mountain retreats in all the towns around these woods, she had to stumble on this one.

She had been incapable of running before, but she managed it now—high, leaping steps across the deep snow, feet barely touching down. She had no idea whether her kidnappers had spotted her staring in at them. She could not risk even the microsecond it would take her to look back over her shoulder. If they were pursuing her, it was silent pursuit, just as her own steps were silent in the muffling powder.

The horror of not knowing created a dread unlike anything she'd ever experienced.

Was that the door? Are they after me?

She harnessed the adrenaline, wallowed in the fear, anything that might pick up her speed and help her get away from that cabin.

The capture, when it came, was so shocking, so devastating, that she almost lost consciousness. Two big hands closed on her shoulders. She literally ran out from under her own body and landed flat on her back in the snow.

His bearded face red with exertion and fury, Spidey tossed her over his shoulder like a rag doll.

Meg screamed her frustration and anger to the sky, pounding her fists against her captor's broad back.

Tiger's smug smile swung into her field of vision. "Well, Margaret, how considerate of you to join us."

13

Dr. Louise Falconer dialed the handset and waited anxiously through the recorded message:

"Hello, you've reached Rufus Sehorn, owner and proprietor of the world-famous bloghog.usa. *Shame on you for phoning when you've got a perfectly good website to visit for news, opinions, and whatnot. But if you really need to speak to me the old-fashioned way, leave a message at the oink."*

Throughout the horrible ordeal of Meg's kidnapping, Sehorn had been a beacon of light in the awful darkness. His sympathy and friendship had been almost as important as the use of his well-known website. His willingness to help them raise three million dollars in ransom money over the Internet was typical of the kind of support he provided. It made perfect sense that, in their most desperate moment, the Falconers would turn to Rufus Sehorn.

The sound of pigs grunting called for her message.

"Rufus, it's Louise. I'm sorry to bother you, but we really don't know where else to turn. Agent Sorenson has gone off somewhere. He says it's about the case, but no one will tell us anything more than that. If you have any news through your site, please call." She hung up.

Her husband put an arm around her shoulders. "Maybe it's not the worst-case scenario. Maybe they've got a real lead, but they don't want to get our hopes up."

She was not comforted. "I don't like the way this is going, John. Two days ago, the FBI had an agent in our house, one on our phones, and two outside. Today it's just a local cop parked across the street. I think the Bureau is closing up shop here. And I'm absolutely terrified about what might have caused that change of heart."

"It makes no sense to panic until we have more information," John insisted. But deep down, he was every bit as frantic as his wife. It didn't help that Aiden had not yet come home. Was it really all because of the weather, or was there something else in play?

It definitely rankled that his son was in the company of Emmanuel Harris. Now Harris had stopped answering his cell phone. It was infuriating and unnerving. Yet John hid those feelings from Louise, not wanting to add to her anxiety.

"Anyway, let's just keep our heads. I'm sure Rufus will call if he hears anything."

The Blog Hog did better than that. He showed up on their doorstep within the hour, his trusty laptop under his arm.

The local officer accompanied the visitor to make sure the Falconers were expecting him.

"This is Rufus Sehorn," Louise explained. "He's welcome here anytime."

Her husband turned to the short, slight blogger with the hobbitlike features. "Tell us you've got something, Rufus. We're losing our minds here."

They sensed right away that Sehorn was bursting with news. His hands trembled as he set up his laptop on the living room coffee table. He fairly vibrated with excitement.

"This just came in this morning," he informed them, bringing up an e-mail.

The Falconers drew close

The time is now. This is your daughter's last chance

Bring the money to the entrance of the old Black River Mine, 3 miles south of Monkwood, Virginia, on County Road 5219

Tonight—5 P.M.

No police, no excuses

NO MERCY

All the color drained from Louise's face. "That's just six hours from now!"

Her husband's voice was shaky. "We'll call Sorenson — forward him the e-mail. It could change his mind about the ransom money."

Louise was in tears. "We can't risk it! If the kidnappers get the slightest whiff of the FBI, they'll kill her!"

"But you don't need the FBI," Sehorn tried to explain. "We *have* the money!"

Both Falconers stared at him.

"It's true," the blogger confirmed. "The site brought in close to four million in pledges. The donors pay by credit card through PayPal. I can have it in an hour, and we can drive straight out there. It'll be tight, but we'll make it."

Meg's father was speechless, overcome by what this odd young man was offering. Ten seconds before, there had been utter hopelessness. Now here was the Blog Hog with a way to bring their daughter home. It was as if a superhero had parachuted in to save the day.

Louise looked worried. "What do we tell the FBI?"

Sehorn regarded her earnestly. "That has to be your decision. But if it was up to me, I'd say nothing at all. Sorenson might try to stop you. He might even ambush the kidnappers by sending agents in before we can get there with the money. It'll get botched just like the last ransom handover. I think it's too risky."

John Falconer nodded. It was all so bizarre — millions of dollars from anonymous online donors, a rendezvous in an abandoned mine, a secret exchange behind the FBI's back. Not even in his Mac Mulvey novels could he ever have imagined something like this. Yet as he racked his trained mind for another way, he knew in his gut that this was their only chance.

His daughter's life. At that moment, it was the only thing that mattered in the world.

He said, "Go ahead and pick up the money."

14

". . . and he's got dark eyes — brown, I think," Mickey was saying into the handset. "And a beard — medium bushy . . ."

Harris paced the hotel room like a caged tiger, listening to his prisoner describing his accomplices over the phone to an FBI sketch artist. Medium bushy! It would be a miracle to identify the other two kidnappers this way, but everything had to be tried.

The room at Blue Valley Lodge had become Harris's base of operations. With the Forest Service out looking for Meg, and the FBI cyber task force tracing the ransom e-mails, the agent had to serve as the nerve center — an inactive role that didn't sit well with the big man.

The room was also a place to warm up and a holding cell for Mickey, who was handcuffed to the bed.

"Do you really think he might try to run away?" Aiden whispered to Harris. "He's sorry about what he did." The prisoner seemed especially harmless in the bright purple SKI VIRGINIA sweatsuit from the gift shop, which had replaced his drenched clothing.

"He'd better pay the Bureau back for that stuff," was the agent's moody reply.

They waited for news that did not come. The FBI tech crew could only report that the ransom e-mails had traveled a path as complex and interconnected as a spiderweb. It would take time to unravel it.

"Time," Harris had told the man, "is something we have very little of."

"Hold on a sec—I think that's call waiting," Mickey said suddenly. He had to pass the receiver to his cuffed hand in order to press the FLASH button. "Hello? . . . Sure, he's right here—Agent Harris, it's the Forest Service."

Harris snatched the handset. "What have you got for me?"

All at once, the big man was fairly exploding with excitement, barking instructions into the phone.

Aiden's heart constricted as if a surgical clamp had been applied to it. "Is it Meg?"

"A chopper detected a heat signature," Harris reported. "They've got rescuers on the way."

Mickey was on his feet now, bouncing up and down, still cuffed to the bed. "Can they see her?"

"Quiet, I'm trying to hear the transmissions from the snowmobile. Wait—they're coming up on the coordinates—"

Aiden clung to Harris's arm. A heat signature — that had to be Meg, didn't it? Who else would be out in two feet of snow?

Please be her . . . please be her . . .

"Oh, no."

The deflation in the agent's voice was a broadsword, slicing into Aiden. He could not bring himself to form the words, but the question hung in the air: *Is she dead?*

Harris let out a long breath. "I understand. . . . Thanks for trying."

"What's going on?" Mickey quavered.

"False alarm. The heat signature turned out to be a bear cub."

Bad news . . . but not the worst. Not yet.

"Forest Service says it's pretty common," the agent went on. "Cubs come out of hibernation, see snow for the first time, and wander off."

"But they'll keep looking, right?" Aiden barely whispered.

Harris nodded soberly. "But once people dig out of the storm, the skiers will be taking advantage of the new powder. Then there'll be heat signatures all over the mountains — too many for the chopper to follow. And when it gets dark —"

Aiden felt sick. The details were different, but what

Harris was describing was all too familiar: a ticking clock.

Time was running out on Meg.

Doctors John and Louise Falconer left their house via the back door. Each had spent more than a year in a maximum-security prison, yet this was the first time either of them had run from the police. They could not allow the officer parked in front of their home to see their departure.

The two criminology professors climbed the fence that separated their yard from the neighbors'. It wasn't easy in their winter coats and heavy boots. Their destination was a place that had just seen two feet of snow.

They crossed the neighbors' property and emerged on the other side of the crescent. There, waiting for them, was Rufus Sehorn, at the wheel of a huge Range Rover.

In spite of his nervousness, John Falconer was curious. "What happened to the Prius?" The Blog Hog normally drove the Toyota hybrid.

"We're going to blizzard country," Sehorn told them. "Only an idiot would try to drive a regular car up there."

Louise's question was a practical one. "Have you got the money?"

She opened the door of the SUV, and her answer lay across the rear seat. She struggled to push the large Samsonite suitcase aside to make room for herself. Her husband got it beside the driver.

"Three million," the Blog Hog confirmed.

"I believe it," she told him. The bag must have weighed sixty pounds. She remembered the duffel of bundled hundred-dollar bills from the previous ransom attempt several days before. It had held two million. The Samsonite was that much heavier.

Sehorn reached around from the front, holding a steaming thermos. "Anybody hungry? I brought pea soup."

The two professors made no reply. It was not out of rudeness. Both felt nothing but friendship and gratitude toward the blogger. But the meeting that would decide whether their daughter would live or die was just a few hours away.

Pea soup was the last thing on their minds.

15

The closer Mike Sorenson got to the mountains, the more the snow piled up. The road had been plowed, but not down to bare pavement. Rock salt, sand, and car traffic had added a layer of icy slush to the mix.

From all sides, towering drifts sent a windblown spray into his Ford Taurus. The car had run out of wiper fluid about fifty miles back. He navigated through a circle of clean glass the size of a Ping-Pong ball, his top speed maybe fifteen miles per hour.

Through the mess, he could see flashing lights. A huge salt truck lumbered ahead, inching along behind a road grader. A figure in yellow coveralls stepped out in front of the Taurus, waving. Sorenson braked to a sliding stop.

He lowered the window, and a woman leaned in. Her hardhat bore the logo of the Virginia Department of Highways. "You're going to want to turn around. There's a gas station about ten miles back where you can get a coffee, maybe a bite to eat."

"Is the road closed?" the agent asked.

"Not officially, but this next stretch is no fun. We've

had some reports of drifting. We're recommending motorists sit out the next few hours."

"Hours?" In agony, Sorenson consulted his watch He'd been traveling since this morning and he'd barely made it to the foothills. A few hours might as well be forever.

"Unless you've got chains or four-wheel drive." She regarded the car dubiously. "Looks like you've got neither."

Sorenson grimaced. The Falconer kidnapping was finally coming to a head. If that little girl was still alive, the chance to bring her home was right now! And where would the case's lead agent be? Stuck at some greasy gas station luncheonette?

Not Mike Sorenson!

He reached into his breast pocket and flashed his badge. "This is official FBI business. I'm ordering you to let me through."

She was unimpressed. "You don't have to order anything. Like I said, the road isn't closed. But you'll want to take it slow. Could be nasty up ahead."

"Thanks for your cooperation." He shut the window and allowed the woman to wave him around the heavy equipment.

Thanks to the salt, a lot of the snow had melted. He steered through several miles of curves, gradually working his way up to a cautious forty miles per hour. He was anxious to get to Blue Valley and take over the investigation from Harris.

The bend wasn't any sharper than the ones that had come before, but it was at the top of a rise, exposed to the wind. Thick, drifting snow covered the highway. Sorenson turned, but the Taurus didn't. The Ford skated off the road and down the slope beyond it. Now he was plunging into the deep ditch, plowing through powder, his foot pressed hard on a brake pedal that was powerless to slow his descent.

And then it was all over. The Taurus sat at the base of a gully, nestled in deep snow.

He put the car in gear. The wheels spun, but there was no traction. The undercarriage rested on so much powder that the tires were well up off the ground. He shifted into reverse. Same result.

Sorenson got out of the car and looked around. High white embankments surrounded him. The snow was pristine except for his own tire tracks. There was nobody around.

"Hello?" he called.

The silence was total.

Agent Mike Sorenson had built his career on going by the rules and following procedure. But try as he might, he could not conjure up a chapter from the FBI manual that covered anything like this.

16

Meg had never learned the names of her three kidnappers. The monikers she gave them came from the masks they had worn on the day of her kidnapping: Spider-Man, Tiger Woods, Mickey Mouse. Spidey, Tiger, and Mickey. The Three Animals.

Two animals, really. Mickey wasn't a part of it anymore. That became obvious in the cabin when Tiger searched Meg and came up with the nail file Mickey had given her.

Spidey's eyes bulged. "That traitor! Didn't I tell you he'd stab us in the back? He was making friends with this little Houdini-girl the minute he laid eyes on her!"

"That's not true!" Meg tried to speak up for Mickey. "He didn't give me that file; it was in my pocket all along! It's not his fault you missed it the first time you searched me!"

Tiger's voice dripped with sarcasm. "And how did you get it from your pocket with your hands bound behind the chair? With mind power?"

"I snuck it out and hid it in my sleeve while you were

tying me up," Meg blustered. It was an obvious lie, but she wanted to take the heat off Mickey. Who knew what kind of revenge the two kidnappers might take on him?

"What are we going to do?" asked Spidey. "We're leaving a ticking bomb out there—a guy who could finger us in a heartbeat."

"Not without fingering himself first," Tiger soothed. "He's weak. He hasn't got the guts to go to the cops. Let him crawl back into whatever hole he came from. That's one less way for us to split the ransom."

Spidey grunted his reluctant assent. It was hard to argue with more money.

"Let's keep our eyes on the ball," Tiger continued. "This is almost over. And that means we're both going to be rich."

Meg's ears perked up. "Almost over?"

"That's right, Margaret," Tiger told her. "If you can behave yourself and not do anything stupid, you'll be back with your family very soon."

Meg nearly choked. Back with her family? Really? These past days—fighting to escape, fighting just to *survive*—she had reached a point where merely staying alive seemed like a long shot. Was it possible that this horrible nightmare might actually be coming to an end?

Tiger supplied more details. "Your parents are on their way right now with the cash."

It was straight out of thin air, completely unexpected. The prospect of a reunion with her family kindled a longing so raw, so powerful that it rendered her helpless — incapable of any action other than waiting and hoping.

Could it be true? She'd been lied to so many times by these criminals.

Tiger smiled at her doubt. "Trust me."

Meg did *not* trust Tiger and Spidey. And obviously, the feeling was mutual, because the next thing Spidey did was tie her to a chair.

Meg's mind was awhirl as he bound her wrists. She wanted to believe that her parents were on the way to buy her freedom. But did it make sense? Where would two college professors come up with three million dollars?

Trussed up like a turkey, she judged time by the progression of shows on the cabin's small TV. It was three and a half interminable hours before Spidey undid the ropes and marched her outside. Tiger was working with a broom, sweeping the snow off something short and squat, with huge tires. It was the ATV — the three-wheeler they had used to chase her in the woods.

"I thought we were waiting for Mom and Dad," Meg protested.

"We're meeting them somewhere else," Tiger told her.

Meg regarded the ATV dubiously. "All three of us will never fit on that thing."

"My Rolls-Royce is in the shop," Spidey growled. "Get on."

A sudden rustling in the nearby trees drew her attention. She looked to the source of the sound, and her hopes evaporated. It was not a potential rescuer, but the bear cub that had shared her shelter during last night's blizzard.

In spite of her disappointment, she felt a surprising surge of warmth. *What a tough little guy to follow me all the way here!*

Spidey noticed the newcomer, too. "Holy—" In a flash, he pulled a pistol from his jacket and squeezed off three quick shots at the cub. The bullets tore through the brush and thudded into tree trunks, missing the target. Frightened, the young bear fled for the cover of deeper woods.

Meg was furious. "Stop it! Stop shooting!"

Tiger was angry for a different reason. "Put the gun away. Do you want to attract every cop in the county?"

Spidey's normally red face was pale behind his beard. "That was a *bear*!"

"It was just a baby," Meg insisted coldly. "Poor guy's just looking for its mother."

"I don't care! I don't like bears!"

"It followed me for miles and never touched me," Meg retorted.

"Let's get moving," Tiger said pointedly. "We don't want to be late."

The three of them were a very tight fit in the ATVs saddle. Meg sat behind Spidey, the driver. Her hands were wrapped around his midsection, her wrists bound together in front of him. To be pressed up against this awful man, unable to move, was beyond torture. Tiger brought up the rear.

As they roared off, Meg's eyes found the spot where the cub had stood before Spidey had opened fire.

We're on exactly the same page, Junior, she reflected grimly. *We're both hoping for a big family reunion.* She couldn't escape the feeling that the creature's chances were much better than her own.

Just inside the edge of the forest, the young bear's natural chase reflex had fixed on the ATV. The animal sprinted energetically after it, bounding easily around trees and through underbrush.

17

When the phone rang, Harris leaped across the hotel room, jostling the room-service cart and upsetting a large carafe of coffee.

"What have you got for me?"

It was Jacobson from the cyber task force. There was progress to report in their remote examination of Spidey's computer.

"We finally unraveled the path the ransom demands followed before they came to bloghog.usa. Let me tell you, those messages were world travelers. They were forwarded through more than two hundred dummy e-mail addresses in thirty-nine countries. Led us a merry chase. Brilliant, really—not amateur night."

"My prisoner said they were working through some kind of web expert," Harris supplied.

"The last stop on the chain was a high-security offshore e-mail account," the tech went on. "The messages went straight from there to the Blog Hog site."

"Whose account is it?" the agent demanded.

"We don't know."

"*When* will you know?"

"It's a problem," the tech admitted. "The e-mail suffix was dot-mc. That's Macao, a small island near Hong Kong. Tricky laws, competing jurisdictions. Not soon. Maybe never."

"So we're nowhere."

"Here's the thing," Jacobson told him, and Harris could hear the man's excitement over the phone. "We found another e-mail. This one didn't come from the confiscated laptop. It went straight from the Macao address to bloghog.usa. Listen: *The time is now. This is your daughter's last chance . . .*"

Breathlessly, Harris reached for a pad and pen and scribbled down the contents of the message.

It was the kidnappers' final instructions to John and Louise Falconer.

Digging a Ford Taurus out of two feet of snow with an ice scraper was like trying to chop down a redwood with a plastic knife. At least it felt that way to Mike Sorenson. Every time he'd shoveled enough to give his tires a chance to find some traction, a suddenly gust would erase much of the past hour's work.

The howling wind abated long enough for him to notice his ringing cell phone. He was only too happy to pause in his labors and answer it.

He heard Emmanuel Harris's voice reading the text of the latest e-mail.

"What are you talking about?"

"That message was sent to the Blog Hog site this morning," Harris explained.

Sorenson was shocked. "You think it means the kidnappers have recaptured the girl?"

"It could be a bluff," Harris admitted. "But bluff or not, it worked. I've been trying to call over to the Falconer house. No answer."

Another gust blew snow in his face. "The parents are on the way there?"

"Couldn't have been hard to get past the squad car at the curb."

"That's not the point," Sorenson said in alarm. "They don't have the ransom money. What do they think the kidnappers will do when they show up empty-handed?"

"Wouldn't be the first time a family got tired of standing around and did something desperate."

Sorenson ignored the barb. "Do we know anything else about the e-mail?"

"It came from the same place as the others — offshore," Harris told him. "Something dot-mc — Macao. Our tech people say it's a dead end. What's your status? How soon before you'll be here?"

"I —" Sorenson hesitated. He didn't want to admit

that he'd driven into a ditch. He'd look like a fool. "The roads are worse than I thought," he said finally. "There's still a lot of snow blowing around." That much was certainly true.

"I can't wait for you," announced Harris. "I've got to get to that mine by five if I can."

"What — without a car?"

"I've got the snowmobile," Harris replied readily. "That's the best way to travel now, anyway."

"But what about your prisoner?" Sorenson persisted. "What about Aiden?"

"They're coming with me. I'll need the prisoner to identify his accomplices. And Aiden — well, you know that kid. Do you honestly think he'd stay put with his whole family mixed up in this?"

The lead agent gestured helplessly with his scraper. He didn't like the idea of Harris doing his job for him. This was going to look horrible to the bosses in Quantico.

On the other hand, five o'clock was fast approaching. If Sorenson couldn't make it to the mine on time, Harris had to try.

"Go."

The Black River mine was located in a deep valley in the mountains a few miles south of the cabins where Meg had blundered herself back into captivity. Fifty years earlier, the place had been a hub of activity. Trucks riding low with heavy loads had lumbered along the access road day and night. Now, decades after the mine had surrendered its last chunk of anthracite coal, that route was unlit and unplowed. Beneath the snow, what was left of the pavement was crumbling.

The sky was still light, but the sun had long since disappeared behind the surrounding hills when the ATV roared into the clearing. It had been a miserable ride with the huge tires churning up a whirlwind of powder. Whatever warmth Meg had been able to store up during her hours in the cabin was gone now. She and her captors were soaked to the skin.

Spidey undid her wrists, and she collapsed into a drift. She was so stiff from being squeezed between the kidnappers that she could barely stand.

He grabbed her by the arm and yanked her roughly to her feet. "Let's go."

Abutting the rock face was a tall structure that looked like a hopper for loading trucks. Spidey dragged her toward the smaller, more dilapidated building beside it. Most of the windows were either missing or broken. There was a sign, but it was so faded that Meg could not make out any of the words except COAL CO.

"A coal mine?" she asked.

"That's not for you to worry about," Tiger said sharply.

It was an eerie spot—isolated, abandoned, forgotten. Whatever hope Meg still harbored that Mom and Dad were on their way faded quickly. This decaying ruin could not be the venue for a happy family reunion.

This is where you come when someone wants you to disappear.

They entered through a battered door that was stuck in the half-open position. It probably used to be the workers' entrance, Meg decided. The outer chamber had once been an office area—there were still a few old desks and filing cabinets. A rear hall led to a locker room. She couldn't tell what was beyond that, but the air inside—dank, cold, stale, and unmoving—told her that the opening to the abandoned mine tunnels could not be far away. It was not the wintry chill coming in from outside. It was a musty, ancient smell—the smell of the belly of the earth.

What future could possibly await her here?

Aiden hung on to the Ski-Doo for dear life, clinging to Mickey, who clung to Emmanuel Harris. A few motorists had ventured onto the road, skidding and sliding as the snowmobile roared past on the unplowed shoulder.

An abandoned mine! The mere thought of it was enough to frost Aiden's blood.

"Don't let your imagination get the better of you," Harris had warned. "It's just a deserted place for the ransom exchange. These things rarely go down in Times Square."

Mickey had fallen for the agent's confident tone, but Aiden hadn't missed the tall man's grim expression, the tightness of the skin around his cheekbones. And there was certainly no mistaking the urgency behind his checkered-flag driving. This was a dire emergency.

There was only one reason to hold a meeting in an old mine, one advantage to such a location — murder.

You can kill somebody and dump the body in miles of underground tunnels where it will never be found.

All at once, the snowmobile's breakneck speed seemed not nearly fast enough.

Waiting.

Meg had never been good at it. Patience was Aiden's strength, not hers. And here, shivering in the steadily darkening office of the old Black River mine, the tension was almost unbearable.

She was not the only one feeling the pressure. Spidey's nervousness mingled with his permanent bad mood to form a toxic cocktail. "Are you sure the Falconers are on their way?" he snapped.

"Everything's going according to plan," Tiger assured him.

"But how do we know? Did you get a phone call?"

She glared at him. "First of all, we're in a coal mine. Do you think there's cell service here? And second, why would I give my number to the enemy? So the FBI could trace it?"

"Did the web guy get in touch with us?" Spidey persisted. "Is that how we know the parents are coming?"

Tiger was exasperated. "Let me worry about that."

"I have a right to be told what's going on! It's my money, too—and my carcass that could go to jail, same as yours!"

"You're not paid to think," she reminded him. "I'm the one who does the thinking around here."

He reddened. "Well, you've done a pretty lousy job of it! You told me this was a simple snatch and trade — the girl for the money, forty-eight hours, tops! That was a week ago — we don't have a penny in our pockets, and every cop alive is after us! We've lost our number three, who could be spilling his guts to the feds right now! And we're standing at the entrance to a hole in the ground, waiting for people who might not even be coming!"

Meg watched, fascinated as her captors argued. It was a clash of the two forces that had tormented her for the past week: Spidey's raw anger versus the cruel intelligence of Tiger's razor-sharp tongue.

"They're coming!" Tiger insisted. "Trust me. If we keep our heads—"

Suspicion edged into Spidey's rage. "That's how you talk to the girl when you've got something to hide."

"Don't be ridiculous," Tiger scoffed.

"You can't know the money's on its way if somebody didn't *tell* you," Spidey pressed on. "Who's working with you? Is it Sean? Have you two got an angle to cut me out of the payday?"

In a whirl of motion, shocking in its swiftness, Tiger

whipped the pistol out of her jacket pocket and pointed it at Spidey's chest. "Don't think I'm afraid to use this!"

Cowed, the burly kidnapper backed up a step.

"You have no idea how I've been looking forward to this moment!" Tiger exclaimed, eyes burning. "This whole week, cooped up with a goon and a fool." She gestured at Meg with the weapon. "*She's* the only one worth respecting — she's a brat, but at least she's got guts!"

"Are you crazy?" Spidey seethed. "What are you doing?"

"You wouldn't have a prayer of comprehending it," she spat at him. "A punch in the face — that's what you understand. You call yourself muscle — the muscle goes all the way to the top of your head!"

Spidey was sputtering with rage. "You'll never pull this off by yourself! What are you going to do? Ride out on that motorized tricycle, juggling three million bucks?"

"Just what I'd expect from a thug like you," Tiger sneered. "Do you honestly believe I'd be crazy enough to strand myself in a place like this with no exit strategy?"

"It's Sean, isn't it? The backstabbing jerk!"

"That idiot? Don't make me laugh!" Tiger regarded him in genuine pity. "You're incapable of seeing the big picture. This is just about money to a small-time hood like you."

Meg's bewilderment matched Spidey's fury. This latest

twist was almost too much for her to process. How had Spidey gone from captor to captive? And who was Sean? Could that be Mickey's real name? Was he in cahoots with Tiger?

No, impossible! Mickey's a good guy now. He helped me escape . . .

But Tiger was telling the truth about one thing: The cunning criminal was far too clever to maroon herself here with no way out.

She has a secret partner—someone to whisk her away when all this is over.

But who? Even more important, if Meg's abduction wasn't about ransom money, then what *was* it about?

She had endured a week of captivity—days of terror and dread, but also excruciating boredom. Most of that idle time she had spent figuring every possible angle of what might happen next.

Yet right then, she didn't have the faintest idea what the coming hours would bring.

Agent Mike Sorenson glistened with snow as he got behind the wheel of his Taurus. He threw the car into low gear and gave it a little gas. The wheels spun, then grabbed. The sedan began to climb the slope in fits and starts.

"Come on," he growled. The tires slipped and caught. He was moving, but backward as well as forward.

In frustration, he gunned the motor. And that turned out to be a mistake.

The car fishtailed on the grade. The front wheels found some traction and plowed out of the shoveled path into deep snow. Sorenson worked furiously at the brakes and gas, but he could not prevent the Taurus from sliding back down into the ditch.

He sat there for a long time, pounding on the steering column, fuming. Who knew how long it would take to get a tow truck to a spot like this on the day after a huge blizzard?

A twelve-year-old girl was in jeopardy. And not just her — now the parents seemed to be involved.

He had a bad feeling about that. Why would two trained criminologists believe that going to a ransom exchange empty-handed could do anything but hurt their daughter's chances?

An odd thought occurred to him: What if they *weren't* empty-handed? He remembered that Rufus Sehorn had been trying to raise money through his website. Was it possible that the Blog Hog had actually managed to come up with three million dollars in just a few days? It seemed farfetched, but anything was possible, especially over the Internet.

There must be some way to find out for sure . . .

Sehorn had mentioned a PayPal account. That meant

PayPal should be able to confirm whether or not a large withdrawal had been made. He dialed the 800-number, and spent a long time on hold, as the company verified that he was the FBI agent he claimed to be. He supplied his badge number to four different PayPal employees, before he found himself on the line with the supervisor on duty.

"It's a collection for the ransom of a kidnapped girl—Margaret Falconer," Sorenson told her. "I need to know if a withdrawal has been made."

He could hear the clicking of a keyboard as the woman searched for the right records. "I don't see anything," she replied finally. "How recent a transaction are we talking about?"

"Within the last twenty-four hours. It would be a large withdrawal—something on the order of three million dollars."

"Three million dollars!" the supervisor blurted. "No, that's quite impossible. I'm showing a balance of just under a thousand."

"Really?" The agent was bewildered. "They were trying to raise three million!"

"That may be so," she told him, "but unless there's a major change in the rate of donations, that kind of money will never be there."

"Are you sure you have the right account? It's a man

named Rufus Sehorn. He might be using his Internet name — Blog Hog."

"We don't have any name at all," the supervisor informed him. "The only contact we have is an e-mail address — *user53418@privacynet.mc*."

It was as if dazzling sun had appeared on the horizon after a long, dark night.

user53418@privacynet.mc

Dot-mc! Macao!

This was the secret address that had been sending the ransom demands to the Blog Hog site! *Rufus Sehorn had been e-mailing himself!*

Barely able to stammer out his thanks, he ended the call. It all made sense.

The Blog Hog was working with the kidnappers!

The elation of solving the puzzle quickly turned to horror. This was vital information. He was the only one who knew it.

And I'm stuck in a ditch.

A priority evacuation — that's what he needed. The FBI manual, however, said a priority evac was only authorized when the agent was in immediate danger. Sorenson had been shaken up. He was cold and wet. He certainly wasn't at death's door.

People's lives are at stake here!

But what about the *rules*? To Mike Sorenson, rules were everything. He had based an entire career on going by the book. No heroics. No running off half-cocked. Just good solid police work. The manual clearly stated —

"To heck with the manual!" he shouted suddenly.

His words were still echoing as he dialed the emergency number.

It was the most difficult ride Dr. John Falconer could remember — tougher, even, than the drive in a steel-clad Department of Corrections bus that had delivered him to federal prison to serve a life sentence.

The thought of his little girl in the custody of desperate criminals was nearly impossible to bear. Yet this — a chance to get her back, but *only* a chance — was pure torture. He reached over the gearshift console to grasp his wife's hand. Their fingers intertwined next to Sehorn's pea soup. But he took no support from her, and her none from him. They were both just too frightened.

At least, Aiden was safe with Harris somewhere. It was their sole comfort.

The Blog Hog tried to be encouraging, and succeeded in driving them insane. "Don't worry, we'll make it there by five. We'll get her back — that's a promise."

The Falconers' gratitude to the blogger was almost without limit. Still, John couldn't help wishing the man would shut up and leave them to their silent agony.

"Look!" Sehorn pointed to a sign as the Range Rover roared past. "Monkwood — twenty miles. We're almost there. Last chance if you want soup."

"No, thank you," Louise managed to croak.

John looked at his watch. Sehorn was right. They really would be there on time. And the rest — that was up to fate.

The highways were snow-covered and slippery, especially the unplowed road that squeezed between two mountains into the valley that was Black River's home. Since the mine hadn't been working in decades, the lane hadn't been properly maintained since then. Overgrown branches scratched at the Range Rover as it bulldozed through the deep powder.

What a place, John thought. He had become skilled at dreaming up settings like this for his Mac Mulvey novels. Now it seemed that a similar imagination was pulling the strings of Meg's ordeal. The idea repulsed him, as if he might be partly responsible for what was happening to his daughter.

He gazed through the windshield at the triple row of tire tracks in the snow ahead of them. The kidnappers?

It had to be. But what kind of vehicle left such a pattern?

His wife peered over his shoulder. "A motorcycle with a sidecar?" she mused aloud.

"Or three motorcycles side by side," suggested Sehorn.

"Impossible," said John. "The tracks are perfectly parallel. Nobody could ride like that."

Rounding the next corner brought the solution to the mystery. There, parked in a small clearing, was the three-wheel ATV. The Falconers looked around, taking in the sight of the loading hopper and entry building jutting out from the rock face.

This was it—the rendezvous location. Whatever Meg's fate, it would happen right here.

"See?" the blogger announced. "I told you we'd make it."

John didn't want to be rude, but Sehorn's cheeriness was nothing short of *crazy*. This was an incredibly dangerous situation, not just for Meg, but also for the three of them. For all they knew, they had walked into a trap, and the kidnappers were about to come out shooting. Why was he treating it like a Sunday drive?

His wife opened the rear door and began to slide the suitcase of money along the leather. "Somebody give me a hand with this—"

Before she could finish the sentence, the heavy piece of luggage toppled off the seat and out of the car. It struck the running board and snapped open.

Louise Falconer emitted a cry of shock. "John—"

John leaped from the car and froze at the sight that greeted his eyes. The bag sat in a drift beside the SUV, its lid sprung wide. The contents spilled out into the snow—twelve copies of the Sunday *New York Times*.

This was the ransom Sehorn had raised over the Internet—that they were about to exchange for their daughter's life.

Not money. Newspapers.

Meg's parents looked to the driver's seat of the Range Rover, but it was empty.

A sharp *click* broke the silence.

The Falconers wheeled. There stood their greatest ally, their only ally, the Blog Hog. In his left hand was his thermos of pea soup. In his right, he held a pistol, pointed straight at them.

19

Although Meg had been told several times that her parents were on their way, the sight of them ducking through the half-open door was overwhelming.

"I can't believe you're really here!" Heedless of the gun that Tiger held on her and Spidey, she ran toward them, arms outstretched. She was just a few feet away from them when the third member of their party entered—a slight, odd-looking man with a very self-satisfied expression on his face. Then she saw his pistol and realized that Mom and Dad were prisoners, too.

The family hug was awkward and nervous.

"What's going on? Who *is* that guy?" Meg asked, bewildered.

"We *thought* he was our friend," her mother replied bitterly.

"You Falconers are really something else," Rufus Sehorn clucked in mock amazement. "After everything that's happened, you still think you have *friends*."

"Who are *you*?" snapped Spidey. "Where's my money?"

The Blog Hog beamed at Tiger. "Congratulations on

your choice of partner. He's every bit the ignorant brute you said he was."

"I told you," she said to Spidey. "This was never about money."

"It was *always* about money!" he bellowed. "There's nothing else for it to be about! Back in Baltimore, we had two million dollars in our hands — till the brother blew it for us!"

"Well, it would have been nice," Sehorn admitted. "We certainly wouldn't have given it back. But we were never planning to hand over the girl. Not for a hundred million."

"If you don't want money, what *do* you want?" John Falconer demanded.

The Blog Hog shrugged. "I would have thought that a couple of college professors might have figured it out by now. Then again, you weren't very hard to fool the first time around."

It all came suddenly clear to Meg. This wasn't a new enemy. It was an old one, dating back to the beginning of the Falconer family's troubles. "HORUS!" she exclaimed in awe. "You're with HORUS Global Group, aren't you?"

Mom and Dad had been framed for helping a terrorist organization. Could that organization have come back to haunt them?

"Very good, Margaret," Tiger approved. "The twelve-year-old is smarter than the parents."

"That's not possible!" Mom protested. "There is no HORUS anymore! They're all either dead or in jail."

"That's exactly what we want the world to think," Sehorn explained pleasantly. "But there are two big fat reminders that HORUS ever existed — the infamous Doctors Falconer. When you're dead, we'll just fade into the fog of old conspiracy theories."

The truth set off a fresh explosion of horror inside Meg. *They kidnapped me so they could murder Mom and Dad!*

Spidey was enraged. "Then what did you need me for? You could have taken out these two on your own — no kidnapping, no nothing!"

"They're too famous for that," Tiger told him. "Their murders would be a front-page story, and HORUS would come under suspicion. It has to look like something different — like a ransom exchange gone bad. The girl, her parents, and one of the kidnappers shot dead in the confusion. No one would even think of HORUS."

Sehorn took a swig from the steaming thermos in his left hand. "Now, wouldn't you have had some of my pea soup," he said to the Falconers, "if you'd known it was going to be your last meal?"

Meg clutched fervently at her parents. Even in the joy

of their release from prison, she had always suspected that her family was doomed to tragedy. The one tiny consolation was that Aiden wasn't here to share in their terrible fate.

As they clung together in this worst of all possible moments, Meg detected a flurry of motion through the cracked and dirty window. The dark fur was sharp against the white of the snow.

The bear cub! It must have followed the ATV!

The animal was nosing its way toward the building, sniffing at the air.

Junior smells the soup!

A desperate plan formed in her mind. If she could lure the cub into the room, it might create enough of a ruckus for her and her parents to escape in the confusion. It was a wild gamble that would probably get them all shot. But at least they would go down fighting.

Without warning, she launched herself at Sehorn and slapped the thermos out of his hand. It hit the floor, sloshing green liquid all over. Startled, the Blog Hog swung his weapon around and took aim at her. He was just about to pull the trigger when a terrified scream was torn from Spidey's throat.

"Be-e-e-ar!!"

The cub was in their midst, bounding around in a clumsy effort to reach the spilled soup. Broad shoulders and flanks bumped into furniture in the tight space, knocking over chairs and tables. The edge of an old wooden desk smacked Tiger in the knee, and she staggered back in pain.

That was enough for Spidey. Left unguarded for the moment, he bolted out of the office and began an awkward high-stepping sprint through the deep snow.

Tiger scrambled to follow. "Don't let him get away!"

She was nearly flattened by a hundred and fifty pounds of flying fur. Hungry as it was, the cub could not resist the instinct to chase a fleeing form. It barreled into the darkening night, jarring the door from its hinges. Seeing himself pursued by the animal he feared, Spidey let out a howl that was hardly distinguishable from the cry of the cub.

In the chaos, John Falconer picked up his daughter and threw her out of harm's way. She hit the floor running, blasting through the locker room area. At the far wall, a low, wide doorway beckoned. And beyond that, blackness.

The mine!

The dark seemed to swallow her. She felt the cold in her bones—not subzero cold, but a dense, dank chill, hanging on air that had not moved in decades. A glance over her shoulder revealed two shapes rushing after her.

"Mom? Dad?"

"*Go!*" her father barked.

She obeyed, pounding deeper into the passage. She was relieved that she and her parents had broken free. But now they were trapped within the rock face, menaced by two armed criminals who were intent on killing them.

How are we ever going to get out of here?

20

Rufus Sehorn hurdled an overturned table and joined Tiger in a mad dash to the locker room. They got there just as John and Louise Falconer fled into the entrance to the mine.

Tiger raised her pistol, but the blogger took hold of her wrist.

"We can't leave them alive!" she exclaimed.

He pulled a small flashlight from his front pocket. "*I'll* go after them. You stand guard here."

"What for?"

"There must be dozens of tunnels back there. They could lose me. But there's only one way out."

Tiger watched him disappear into the black hole of the mine. Everything they'd worked for — the entire future of HORUS — depended on the elimination of the Falconers.

It had to go exactly right.

The light was already fading as the Ski-Doo's treads tore into the unplowed road that led to the Black River mine.

Hanging on at the rear, Aiden leaned out as far as he dared, peering past Mickey and Harris into the bright cone projected by the headlight.

It's already past five; the meeting could be over . . .

Aiden didn't want to think about what that might mean.

Suddenly, he was bellowing, *"Stop! Go back!"*

Harris jerked hard on the handlebars, and the snowmobile swung into a tight quarter-turn. They skidded thirty feet before the skis dug in, and the craft lurched to a halt.

"What is it?" the agent demanded.

"Look!" Aiden pointed, his eyes wide with horror.

It was barely visible in the shadowy dusk. The white of the snow, and then a different color — darker —

Red.

"Blood!" Mickey croaked.

As they approached the crimson stain, Aiden felt the stomach-numbing weightlessness of free fall.

Don't let it be Meg. . . . Don't let it be Meg. . . .

A stocky, bearded man lay at the center of the discoloration.

Aiden turned away. It was not a pleasant sight. Spidey's clothing was torn and blood-spattered. *Too much blood . . .*

"It's Joe," Mickey said in a strangled voice. "I mean — that might not be his real name — "

Harris bent low over the victim. "He's still breathing—barely."

"Is he shot?" Aiden asked.

The FBI man shook his head. "Some kind of animal attack, I'd say. Bear or mountain lion." The snow was too powdery to hold distinct footprints, but the tracks seemed to be large. "Bear, probably. Let's keep our eyes open. That thing can't be too far away."

Aiden was amazed. With all the grave dangers attached to a ransom exchange, a bear attack was the furthest thing from his mind.

"What are we going to do?" asked Mickey. "He needs a doctor."

Harris pressed handfuls of fresh snow onto Spidey's many wounds. "The cold helps slow the bleeding," he explained. The gash on the kidnapper's shoulder continued to ooze, so the agent wrapped it with his scarf. "Best we can do. We've got innocents to worry about."

They cleared a small opening in the snow and propped Spidey against a tree.

"Shouldn't we tie him up?" asked Aiden.

"If he comes to, he won't be running any marathons," Harris decided.

The three got back on the snowmobile and continued down the road, driving slowly, cautiously. Surely, the mine had to be close; otherwise, Spidey could not have reached this spot on foot. Aiden stared into the halogen glare with wide-eyed intensity. The possibility that Meg — and maybe Mom and Dad, too — might be just around the next corner was an electric current, pulsing through him.

They had only been moving for a few minutes when Rufus Sehorn's Range Rover appeared in the headlight beam. Harris shut down the Ski-Doo, and the three of them pushed it into the cover of some brush.

"Keep behind me," the agent instructed Aiden and Mickey. "And don't make a sound."

They stayed close to the hillside as they approached the SUV, Harris in the lead. All at once, he flattened himself against the rock face.

He beckoned to Mickey and whispered, "Is that the other kidnapper?" He guided the young man's gaze slowly around the curve of the stone.

Tiger stood just outside the doorway to the mine building. Mickey recognized her profile instantly — and also the shape of the pistol in her hand.

He retreated to face Harris. "That's her — Marcelle."

"What can you tell me about her?" Harris probed. "Do you think she'd harm a hostage if I make a move?"

"It's too risky!" Aiden hissed.

Mickey looked anxious. "I don't think there's anything she wouldn't do."

Harris hesitated. It was a tough call—even for a seasoned agent. "We can't just wait here forever."

"There's another way," said Mickey. He ran out from the safety of the hillside, waving his arms and bellowing, *"Marcelle!!"*

Tiger was immediately alert, gun at the ready. "Who's there? How do you know my name?"

Mickey raised his hands but did not stop until he was directly in front of her. "It's me—Sean!"

Tiger stared at him as if she were seeing a ghost. "How did you get here?"

"By snowmobile!" he told her. "I'm back—I'm here to help!"

Aiden watched, stunned. "Is he selling us out?"

"I don't think so," murmured Harris, transfixed.

"Then what's he doing?"

"Don't move!" the agent ordered Aiden. He scrambled up the hillside, his boots slipping in the snow.

Mickey's arrival had caught Tiger off guard. "How did you know where to find me? You were back at the cabin when we picked this place!"

"The laptop!" Mickey told her. "I read the e-mail!"

Tiger's voice was shaky. "The e-mail never came from that laptop!" She was used to being in control. This unexpected arrival flustered her.

"We traced it—" Mickey tried to explain.

"Who's we?" she demanded. "The police?"

"No — I went on the Internet. I found — "

"You couldn't find sand at a beach! You went to the cops!"

"No — "

Aiden watched in a mixture of fascination and dread. He kept one eye on Harris, who was nearing the top of the rock face. Would he reach Tiger in time?

"Where are they?" she stormed. "Did you bring them here?"

Mickey was beyond speech now, hypnotized by the barrel of Tiger's gun.

"Answer me!" She cocked back the hammer.

Acting purely on impulse, Aiden bounded into the clearing. *"Hey!"*

Tiger wheeled, bringing the pistol to bear on him.

From the top of the rise, a tall figure dropped twelve feet, landing with a clatter on the roof of the structure behind Tiger. The noise drew her attention from Aiden. She spun around just as Harris jumped.

He descended on her from above, slamming his clasped hands on the base of her neck. Agent and kidnapper collapsed to the snow.

Meg fled through the mine, stumbling over fallen rocks and old railroad tracks. The darkness surrounding her was near total. She could see nothing but dim points of light, spiraling in the black.

Fireflies?

Something like damp, papery rubber slapped at her cheek. She windmilled her arms in front of her, and that was when she felt them. Bats—their rodent eyes glowing all around her.

Wheezing, she fought to control her revulsion. *They can't hurt you. Worry about the things that can.*

Two armed criminals were after her and her parents. Tiger and—who was that other guy?

He wants you dead. That's all you need to know.

She reached out to feel her way through the passage and jumped back. The wall came to an angle as the tunnel split in two.

There's more than one tunnel!

The possibility had not occurred to her before that moment.

What if I get lost? Or if Mom and Dad do?

Where *were* her parents? They had been not too far behind her. But she could no longer hear their footfalls.

"Mom?" she called in a low voice. "Dad?"

The response was a flash of orange light, the crack of a pistol, and the deadly whine of a bullet slicing through the mine.

21

At the sound of gunfire, Aiden and Mickey raced to the scene of the collision in front of the doorway.

"Agent Harris!" Aiden cried.

"I'm okay." With a groan, the tall man lifted himself off Tiger. The female kidnapper lay motionless in the snow, knocked out cold. From a ski suit pocket, Harris produced a set of handcuffs and shackled her to the rusted grill of a broken window.

"But who was shooting?" asked Mickey.

Three pairs of eyes peered through the office area to the locker room and the darkness beyond.

"Meg!" gasped Aiden, sprinting inside.

"Come back!" Harris ordered to no avail. He collared Mickey, who was attempting to follow Aiden. "Go to the Range Rover. See if you can get the high beams on. We've got to find a way to light up that mine."

Aiden galloped across the locker room and sprawled headlong through the entrance to the tunnel.

Wham!

The sudden explosion of pain was so devastating that he saw bursts of bright color as he collapsed to the floor, dazed.

All at once, the outer building lit up behind him. It cast just enough glow into the passage to see what he'd hit.

The ceiling! It was so low that he had smacked his head on a shoring timber. He scrambled up and continued in a hunched position.

As he pushed onward into the dwindling light, he tried to piece together what had happened. He'd seen the Range Rover, but not the smaller three-wheeler parked beyond it. So he was guessing that the kidnappers had brought Meg in the SUV. He assumed that his parents hadn't arrived yet, or perhaps weren't coming at all. Harris had never been positive about that.

The bear attack, though, was straight out of left field. Bad luck — or maybe good luck. It might have provided the diversion that had allowed Meg to escape into the mine. But someone was in there with her — someone with a gun.

A fourth kidnapper? Someone even Mickey doesn't know about?

The tunnel split into side passages and crosscuts. It grew darker with every step away from the entrance. He had to risk calling out, if only to let his sister know she wasn't alone.

"Meg!" He was shocked at how his voice reverberated through the underground maze.

Just as absolute black seemed to be closing in on him, he noticed a dim flickering in the tunnel ahead.

A flashlight!

Its warm glow was almost as welcome as the swelling of hope in his heart. He raced for it, knowing the odds were fifty-fifty that he was running toward the unknown gunman. At least part of him understood that this was not a wise move. But he could not — would not — pass up a chance to bring his little sister out of this nightmare. He made a wrong turn, blundering down a crosscut into a side chamber. But when the glimmer disappeared, he knew to retrace his steps until he saw it again.

He followed the tunnel around at a jog and froze, shielding his eyes. The sudden onslaught of the torch was so brilliant that he was momentarily blinded.

A voice — definitely not Meg's — said, "Aiden?"

"Rufus?" Aiden managed enough of a squint to make out the Blog Hog's slight form about forty feet ahead. "What are you doing here?"

"I came with your parents," Sehorn replied.

"Mom and Dad? Where are they?"

"We got separated," the blogger told him. "This place is like a rabbit warren!"

"And Meg's in the mine somewhere?"

"We'll find her together," Sehorn decided. "It's too dangerous for you to be wandering around without a flashlight."

"We've got to hurry," Aiden hissed urgently. "There's a fourth kidnapper around somewhere, and he's got a gun!"

"Clever boy." Sehorn raised his weapon and took careful aim.

It was fugitive instinct—survival instinct. Aiden slammed himself against the rock wall just as the Blog Hog pulled the trigger.

The noise was deafening. The report of the pistol seemed to crack between Aiden's ears. The bullet whistled past him down the tunnel.

He took off, his bewilderment rivaling his terror. Why was the Falconer family's biggest supporter shooting at him? Pebbles from the ceiling rained down on his head and shoulders as he ran. One stone chunk was large enough to hurt, yet he knew that nothing was as dangerous as the next shot from Sehorn's gun.

Another blast resounded in the mine, but Aiden was already flinging himself through the opening to the side chamber. He stumbled on some steel tracks, went down, and somersaulted up again without missing a step. All his efforts were now focused on a single goal: escape from Rufus Sehorn.

The fourth kidnapper—the Blog Hog. An enemy pretending to be their friend. Total, utter betrayal.

Aiden could see a little here, but that was just a reminder of how much peril he was in. The light was coming from Sehorn's flashlight, a bobbing glow that meant death was not far behind him.

He scrabbled along, pawing the stone walls, taking every fork and detour. He was losing himself in the mine, seeking the cover of velvety blackness.

One thought sustained him: *If I'm going to save Meg, first I have to save myself.*

Meg was getting better at feeling her way through the dark, probing with her hands as she shuffled her feet forward.

More difficult than moving was controlling her panic. Her brief joy at seeing her parents was now turned to a terrible dread for their lives. They were being hunted just as she was, and she had no way to help them, or even find them. They were all at the mercy of Tiger and that horrible little man—two HORUS killers.

HORUS. So that was what her kidnapping had really been about—to lure Mom and Dad out of the spotlight so they could be quietly executed. And HORUS would go on supporting terrorists, far from the public eye.

Meg's plan, if you could call it that, was to draw the killers deeper into the mine, and then somehow sneak past them, find Mom and Dad, and make a break for it. It was a thousand-to-one shot—maybe a million to one—but her experience as a fugitive had taught her never to give up.

When she bumped up against the obstacle, she knew instantly that this was not merely the dead end of a tunnel. The walls of the passages were semi-smooth rock. This was a pile of rubble, ranging from pebbles to boulders. An old cave-in.

The thought chilled her. She had heard stories of miners trapped deep within the earth, locked in claustrophobic blackness as the air ran out.

She was backing away along the smooth wall when she heard something that brought her back to her own far more immediate problem.

Two gunshots.

Her mind reeled. They weren't aimed at her. Who, then? Were those the shots that had made her and her brother orphans?

This time, fear was a smaller part of her reaction—an explosion of anger and a determination to protect her family. She flailed blindly in search of some sort of club. It came to her hands almost at once. The cave-in had dislodged some shoring timber, and here was a jagged piece of wood roughly the size of a baseball bat. She snatched it up and headed back where she'd come from.

Feeling her way with one hand and brandishing the weapon with the other, she stalked through the passage. The decision to fight rather than fly may not have been smart, but it definitely felt right.

When the collision came, it was a complete shock. Whoever hit her must have been running. She bounced off, landing flat on her back, and heard the other person fall, too.

This is it!

She scrambled up and reared back with her timber to deliver the home run swing.

Her attacker lunged at her. Arms locked around her midsection, and her blow missed. She tried to break free by bringing the wood straight down on the bear hug that held her. She struck something solid, and a voice cried, *"Ow!"*

A very familiar voice.

"Aiden?"

He held her so tightly she could hardly breathe.

22

The mine's low ceilings had been a problem for the others, but for Emmanuel Harris they were a virtual impossibility. Bent almost double, he navigated by flashlight, straining to pinpoint the location of the echoing gunshots. But who could tell how sound might travel in a place like this?

In the midst of his discomfort, he was aware that his actions had been very un-FBI. The three kidnappers were outside the mine, while he was inside. And he'd allowed Aiden to lose himself in a danger zone where there was shooting. In the past few days, Harris had bent more rules and disobeyed more instructions than Mike Sorenson ever would in twelve careers. But there were lives on the line, and that was all that mattered.

As he stepped into the intersection of two tunnels, he shone his flashlight as far as it would go in every direction. In the corridor to the right, the beam swept across a single fleeing boot.

In an instant, he was off and running in an ostrichlike gait, his neck stretched forward.

"FBI!"

He ducked down the crosscut, and there they were, cowering in the light of his torch — John and Louise Falconer.

"Have you seen Aiden?" Harris demanded.

"Aiden?" Louise echoed. "You brought Aiden *here?*"

"It's a long story," Harris said impatiently. "Where's your daughter?"

"Somewhere in the mine!" John explained in agitation. "We lost her! He was chasing us — and shooting!"

"Who?" Harris barked. "Who was shooting?"

"Rufus Sehorn!"

"The Blog Hog?" Harris was thunderstruck. Yet he had never quite trusted the odd young man.

"He's with HORUS," Louise explained tearfully. "That's what all this was from the start — a plot to get rid of us and make it look like a botched kidnapping."

"HORUS," the agent repeated. A sinister name he'd believed to be in the past.

"Please save our children!" Louise begged.

Harris pointed back in the direction he'd come from. "Two lefts and a right, then follow the headlights from outside. I'll look for the kids."

"We're coming with you," John said immediately.

The FBI man had expected nothing else. He was getting used to these Falconers. They did not shy away from anything. And they *never* followed instructions.

"All right," he said with a sigh. "Stay behind me. And no talking."

For Aiden and Meg, the reunion was short. So much had happened to each of them in the past week. But there was no time for storytelling. Just as it had been in their fugitive days, once again everything had come down to survival.

As they compared notes, their situation began to look bleaker and bleaker. Wandering in a labyrinth of underground tunnels . . . pursued by the Blog Hog . . . Mom and Dad lost, or worse.

They held hands as they walked — not for support, but to keep from losing each other. Visibility was absolute zero, like being wrapped in endless black drapery.

"Why did you have to come here, Aiden?" Meg blurted miserably. "At least one of us could have been away from this mess!"

He was irritated by her attitude. "Shut up, Meg. You'd have done the same thing and you know it."

They fell silent, both amazed that they could find

something to bicker about when there was so little time and so much information they needed to share. Meg had never even heard the names Mike Sorenson and Rufus Sehorn. And she told him of her three kidnappers and how Mickey had helped her escape.

"He's on our side now," Aiden updated her. "The other two are out of the picture. The one with the beard is in bad shape. Harris says it was a bear attack."

Meg was dubious. "A bear was chasing him, but it was just a cub."

"Well, it must have been some cub. You should have seen that guy — it was like he'd been mauled by a T. rex! The blood —"

"Aiden!" she hissed suddenly.

"Yeah?"

"I can see you."

He squinted into the gloom. It was still very dark, but he could distinctly make out his sister's features several inches away. And that meant —

"There's a light around here somewhere," he whispered.

They froze, watching and listening. The glow was diffused, pooling ahead of them at an intersection. They could hear faint shambling footsteps.

Aiden and Meg exchanged uncertain glances. It could

be Harris and help, but also Sehorn and death. Running away might save their lives, but it could also cost them their chance at rescue.

It was worse than indecision. They were paralyzed as the light grew brighter.

We're blowing it! Aiden thought in agony. How many times had their lives depended on split-second action? Yet he found he could not make this call, the most important one of all. He looked at his sister — younger, but tougher and gutsier. She had never failed to rise to every challenge. But now she was frightened and exhausted, cowering next to him. Whatever their fate, it would be out of their hands.

When the light exploded around the corner, it was like a sunburst, spectacular and blinding. Aiden couldn't see the figure behind the torch, but he knew it was too short to be Harris.

When the first shot came at them, it wasn't even a surprise. The bullet whizzed dangerously close to Aiden's shoulder and struck behind them with a metallic clang. Both Falconers wheeled.

A small, narrow-gauge coal car sat there on a rusted siding. There was a pockmark on the front where the slug had struck and ricocheted off.

With a single mind, brother and sister were galvanized into motion. Another shot whined past as they sprinted for the wagon and dove inside, ducking as low as they could get. Four more bullets slammed into the metal walls, bouncing in all directions. The sound filled the tunnel like a violent thunderstorm.

"We're sitting ducks!" Meg gasped. "All he has to do is walk over here!"

And then a deep voice from far away boomed, *"Se-horn!"*

Aiden's heart leaped. Harris! The agent had found them.

The firing continued, but in the opposite direction. Now Sehorn was shooting at the man from the FBI.

The pungent smell of gunpowder filled the passage. And something else—a coarse pebbly dust descending from above.

Meg squeezed her brother's arm. "Aiden—listen!"

He felt it as much as heard it. The noise was separate from the gunfire—an intense grinding that set his teeth on edge, and raised a nameless horror inside him.

"Run!"

The two scrambled out of the coal car and took off down the passage away from the battle.

Weakened by shock waves and ricocheting bullets, the ceiling gave way behind them. With a monumental roar, hundreds of tons of rock came pelting down and filled

the passage. Rufus Sehorn disappeared under an ava-
lanche of crushing rubble. The coal car was buried as the
earth reclaimed the tunnel.

The world went dark.

Harris bounded through the collapsing passage, one
arm around John Falconer, the other gripping Louise.
Dust choked them — dust and the terrible realization of
what had happened.

The Falconers ran for their lives but had no interest in
living. They had just witnessed their two children buried
alive.

Meg must have lost consciousness for a moment—but only a moment—because the air was still full of pulverized rock, and the rumble of the cave-in had not yet died away. She was flat on her face on the ground, partially covered in debris.

"Aiden—"

"Right here." The voice was close to her ear.

She shook off the loose stones and struggled to her feet. Her outstretched arm encountered nothing but tons of shattered rock where the tunnel had once been. All light had vanished, along with any sound from the other side of the pile. They were sealed in an underground tomb.

Aiden was at her side. "If the collapse had gone on for a few more feet, we would have been crushed like Rufus."

"Lucky us." Meg's voice was hollow.

Aiden grasped at a medium-size boulder. Grunting with effort, he rolled it aside. The motion touched off a minor rockslide that filled the empty place with at least three times as much rubble.

"Don't," Meg ordered sharply. "That HORUS guy must have been fifty feet away. And who knows how long the cave-in goes on the other side of him? It would take years to dig out of here. We'll starve before that. Or die of thirst or suffocation."

She felt him nod. This, then, was how it was going to end. The Falconer way—separation, heartbreak, tragedy. Mom and Dad were out of prison but locked away from their children. Aiden and Meg were reunited but doomed.

"I'm sorry I couldn't find you before it was too late," Aiden croaked, his voice hoarse with dust and emotion.

She searched for something to say, something that might bring them both comfort—as if anything could. Bereft of words, she wrapped her arms around him.

They clung to each other. Surely, no two siblings had ever been through so much together. It had been a life-and-death roller coaster from the moment of their parents' arrest. But now it was clear that the ride was over. It was almost a relief to give up the struggle.

And then a strand of her hair blew across Aiden's cheek.

"Meg—"

"I felt it, too!" she exclaimed.

They were trapped in a collapsed tunnel deep inside a mountain. Where was fresh air coming from?

"An air shaft!" Aiden exclaimed in wonder. "They drilled them in these old mines so the workers could breathe!"

"But how do we find it?" Meg urged. "It's pitch-black in here!"

Aiden unzipped a pocket of his ski suit and pulled out a tissue. He peeled off and discarded a layer, then tore a thin strip of the fine gauzy paper. He held it up with one hand and checked the result with the other. It hung limp for an instant, and then began to flutter against his fingers. He took a step in the opposite direction of the airflow.

He nudged Meg. "This way. Move slowly. Don't create any breeze."

"What are we doing?"

"Shhh. I made a wind sock."

Slowly — agonizingly slowly — they backtracked the air current toward its origin. More than once they were forced to stop and wait for the Kleenex to catch another draft. The movement of that flimsy scrap of tissue bore the weight of any chance of a future for Aiden and Meg Falconer.

It took a long time that seemed even longer. They shuffled deeper into the mountain in search of the source of the hope-giving wind.

"Wait—" Aiden rasped suddenly. "I lost it."

They stood still, scarcely daring to breathe. Nothing.

"Oh, no!" moaned Meg. "What did we do wrong?"

All at once, a cool draft tickled the hair on top of her head. She looked up. Was it real, or were her eyes fabricating what her heart yearned to see? A single faint star twinkled down at her.

They hadn't lost the air current—they were standing directly underneath the shaft!

She felt around the mine ceiling and reached into the opening. Her fingers closed on a cold metal rung, fastened onto the rock.

"Give me a boost."

He heaved her from below, and she was delighted to find a series of rungs leading up the airshaft.

"We are *so* out of here! Come on!"

The two began to climb, carefully testing each bar before putting any weight on it. They ascended through the lightless passage, their elbows and shoulders bumping up against a conduit that was barely two feet wide.

Whenever the claustrophobia threatened to overwhelm Meg, she would tilt her head, and there it would be—the star, beckoning from above. The air seemed purer and colder. It smelled like freedom.

"Bro, you are a *genius*," she called down to Aiden. "How'd you think of the wind sock?"

"The Alaska Pipeline Caper," Aiden puffed.

"You mean Mac Mulvey? Why don't I know that one?"

"Dad never finished it," her brother replied. "He was still working on it when he and Mom got arrested. Mulvey's trapped inside a sealed pipe . . ."

The explanation went on, but Meg was no longer listening. There were three stars visible now, and she could clearly see where the black shaft gave way to lighter sky. She climbed faster, her arms and legs powered by the thought that they were actually going to make it.

Then she was out, scrambling into the deep snow and turning to give her brother a hand.

At last, the two of them were standing on the slope, laughing as if someone had just told the most hilarious joke in the world. Meg wracked her brain for an explanation of what was so funny, but all she could come up with was: *We're alive!*

Below them, through the trees, they could see the clearing in front of the mine, lit by the Range Rover's headlights.

"Let's get down there!" Aiden exclaimed excitedly.

Meg did not have to be asked twice.

They descended the hillside as if the two feet of fresh powder didn't exist. About halfway there, Aiden spotted their parents.

"Mom and Dad! They're okay!"

Their pace doubled. Both were running full out now, scrambling, stumbling, and kicking up an enormous cloud of snow.

"We're here!" Meg shrieked. "Mom! Dad!"

They jumped to the road and rounded the bend to the clearing, plowing through the drifts.

A wail of recognition burst from Louise Falconer, and suddenly the parents were rushing toward them. Harris was right behind them. And who was that? Mickey! Meg couldn't believe she was actually glad to see him again.

Most amazing of all, a dark bundle of fur shot from a stand of trees and made straight for Meg — the bear cub, seeking out its old friend.

Meg slowed up. "Hold your horses, Junior. Keep your distance."

Aiden frowned. "You're right, Meg. It really *is* just a cub."

A second animal rose from all fours out of the same thicket, and this one was no cub. It was a fully grown black bear, easily eight feet tall, ready to do battle to protect its baby.

Aiden's description of Spidey's injuries sprang to Meg's mind: *He looks like he was mauled by a T. rex.* There was no question that this was the closest thing to a T. rex anyone was going to find in the state of Virginia.

Aiden and Meg stood like statues, willing the cub to back off.

If it leaves, Meg prayed, *surely the mom'll leave, too. . . .*

The huge bear advanced, plainly angry. A single swipe of its powerful paw might rip a person's head clean off. Their escape from the mine was turning into a meaningless victory. This horror was greater than a killing bullet, or even a slow death in a dark tunnel. They were facing the mindless violence of a wild animal.

Agent Emmanuel Harris of the FBI used his long legs to leap forward and place himself between the Falconer kids and the bear. His gun was pointed, but he didn't dare use it except as a last resort. Anything less than a perfect shot would bring disaster down on all of them.

"Back away, nice and slow," he tossed over his shoulder at Aiden and Meg.

"I don't know if that'll work," Meg quavered. "The cub has been following me—"

"Will you do as you're told just this once?"

The exchange agitated the mother bear. With a howl of fury, it drew back a massive paw. Just as the lethal claws were about come down on Harris, a brilliant light from above flooded the clearing, and a wild wind whipped up the snow. The clatter of rotor blades was deafening, and a large transport helicopter began to descend into their midst.

The terrified bear cub scurried into the woods. And, after a few seconds of indecision, the mother dropped down to all fours again and loped off after it.

The chopper set down, and out bounded Agent Sorenson. He found his victim rescued, the kidnappers in custody, and the ringleader buried under tons of rock.

Another case solved by Mike Sorenson.

FALCONER DAUGHTER SAFE
AFTER MINE RESCUE

MONKWOOD, VA—AMALGAMATED WIRE SERVICE:
In a showdown straight out of Hollywood, involving gunfire and a collapsing mine, federal agents rescued Margaret Falconer, 12, who had been missing for nine days. The incident at the abandoned Black River mine in western Virginia uncovered a plot by the notorious HORUS Global Group, a front for international terrorists. What was believed to be a straight kidnapping turned out to be an attempt by HORUS to eliminate Doctors John and Louise Falconer and have the murders blamed on a ransom exchange gone wrong. The Falconers are the noted criminologists who served fourteen months in prison for aiding HORUS until they were proven innocent earlier this year.

In a bizarre twist, the mastermind of HORUS's plan was revealed to be Rufus Sehorn, 29, better known as the Internet's popular Blog Hog. Sehorn was killed in the cave-in, buried under the collapsed rock ceiling. Mining experts say his body may never be recovered.

Charged with kidnapping, attempted murder, and treason is Sehorn's accomplice, Marcelle Devereaux, 34. Two others are implicated in the kidnapping, but not the HORUS plot. Joseph McFadden, 27, faces fifteen to twenty-five years in prison for his role in the abduction. He is currently in serious but stable condition in Alberta County medical center after a bear attack unrelated to the rescue. Sean Michael Antonino, 20, is cooperating with the authorities, who say he played a major role in bringing the Falconer girl home alive.

"This proves beyond a doubt that there never was any collaboration between the Falconer family and HORUS," said Emmanuel Harris, the FBI agent who originally arrested the Falconers and who was on the scene for last night's rescue. "It's time to leave these poor people alone, once and for all."

John Falconer opened the front door to find Harris on the stoop, an extra-large coffee steaming in his extra-large hand.

"You're not reading your own press, Agent Harris. We're supposed to be left alone, remember?"

"Sorry to disturb you," Harris mumbled. "It's Aiden I'm here to see."

A head peered out of the kitchen. "Hey, Agent Harris!" Aiden bounded into the room, obviously glad to see the visitor. "Did you get your car back?"

"Eventually." Harris sighed. "The snowmobile ran out of gas. I won't bore you with the details. How's your sister?"

"Bouncing back," Aiden replied. "She and Mom are out shopping for a belated birthday present." He noticed the jacket and baseball cap the big agent was carrying. They belonged to Richie Pembleton, Aiden's best friend. When Aiden had run away to search for his sister, he had disguised himself in the clothes Richie always wore.

"Thanks a lot," Aiden exclaimed. "Richie loves that hat. I don't think he could have lived without it."

"It's all part of the service." Harris grinned.

Aiden's father noted the genuine friendship that seemed to have formed between his son and the hated government agent who had caused their family so much grief. He took a deep breath. It was difficult for him to say this, but it needed to be said.

"Agent Harris, when I wake up in the morning, the first thing I see on the inside of my eyelids is you putting yourself between our kids and a rampaging bear. How can my wife and I ever repay you for that?"

"Well, for one thing" — Harris shuffled uncomfortably, glancing down at his size-fifteen shoes — "you could try to forgive me."

Dr. Falconer was taken aback. "Forgive you?"

This time, the agent met his gaze.

"And that means so much to you?" John persisted.

Harris nodded silently.

When Meg and her mother clattered into the house a few minutes later, laughing and laden with packages, an unexpected sight greeted them in the front hall—John Falconer and Emmanuel Harris, longtime enemies, engaged in a solemn handshake.

EPILOGUE

For Meg, the biggest difference in her life now was how much she appreciated freedom. It was something she'd never thought about—not before she'd been locked in car trunks and storerooms and cellars, and tied to chairs. Now, with every step she took, she swung her arms a little higher, just to prove that she could. Every time she fastened her seat belt, she kept her hand on the buckle—a reminder that she could open it any time she chose. All small changes that nobody noticed except Meg herself.

Which might explain why no one at her middle school ever figured out who released the frogs from the science lab into the marshy grass behind the playground.

Only someone who had suffered captivity could understand the sweetness of freedom.